I0627679

DUPED

Atlantic City's Most Wanted #4

Charity Parkerson

Punk & Sissy Publications

Copyright

—Warning: This book is intended for readers over the age of 18. Some of my books contain allusions to past abuse and trauma.

Copyright © 2025 Charity Parkerson

Editor: BZ Hercules & Consultants

CONTENTS

INTRODUCTION

*A BOY ON THE **hunt for a sugar daddy. A dangerous man with a deadly obsession. Nothing good can come of them.***

Portland spent years scheming to own the man of his dreams. He did everything within his power to corner his obsession. All of that hard work was for nothing and now he's left bitter and looking for an outlet for his rage. A tiny poker dealer with a sassy smile will do as well as anyone.

When Tarek moved to Atlantic City, he had one goal in mind: to find an older, richer man to sweep him away. He's had his eye on Portland for a while, but the guy hasn't noticed before now. Tarek has his attention, and he's not letting go, even if it costs him everything. With Portland, and all his secrets, that's a reality that might very well come to fruition.

Duped is the fourth book in Charity Parkerson's Atlantic City's Most Wanted series. These are sexy and sometimes dark stories where the richest and most dangerous men in Atlantic City meet their match. These are best enjoyed when read in order.

CHAPTER ONE

PORTLAND WALES. TAREK HAD been watching him for a while. The guy threw money around like it meant nothing, especially on substantially younger men, supposedly...or one in particular, anyhow. Rumor had it that much younger man had recently married. Tarek figured that left an open position in Portland's life. Tarek wanted the job. That was why he had purposely left his bag at his dealer's station when shifts changed, and he saw Portland headed his way. Tarek bade his time and grabbed a couple of drinks before heading toward an accidental meeting. He squeezed into the space next to Portland at the table, doing his best to get in close while not appearing to do so on purpose.

"Sorry. I left my bag."

The new dealer glanced below the table and found Tarek's small, clear plastic tote bag. He passed it Tarek's way. Tarek turned his head, bracing himself for anything.

Light blue eyes were locked on him in a dark and hungry way that immediately had goosebumps skirting his skin. Tarek worked up his sweetest smile. "Excuse me. I didn't mean to invade your space." Without waiting for a response, Tarek walked away. He knew it was a risk, but the first encounter was in the books. Next time they saw each other, this gave Tarek an excuse to strike up a conversation. Seduction was a slow and perfectly timed game.

"Excuse me. I think you dropped this."

Tarek glanced behind him. Portland was hot on his heels. Shock had Tarek freezing in his tracks. This wasn't how he pictured things. "I'm sorry. Are you talking to me?"

A congenial smile, completely at odds with his earlier dark expression, met Tarek's question. "Yes. You dropped this."

Tarek's gaze reluctantly moved from Portland's gorgeous eyes to the item he held. It was a stack of bills. Tarek blinked. It was likely a few thousand dollars.

A nervous laugh escaped Tarek. It was completely genuine. He felt like he was the one who had stepped into a trap. "No. Sorry. I definitely didn't drop that."

Portland stepped closer. Something flashed in his eyes that had Tarek's mouth going dry. "I promise you did."

A thought hit Tarek. He cocked his head to one side and eyed Portland. "Sir, are you trying to buy me?"

Portland's stare briefly moved to Tarek's mouth before returning to hold his gaze. "What if I am?"

A smile exploded across Tarek's lips. This definitely wasn't going the way he planned, but he could adapt. Tarek was good at thinking on his feet. "You know, if you had simply asked me to dinner, I would've said yes." He turned away.

Tarek bit back a smirk. He would definitely have a way to strike up the next conversation. Tarek made it three steps before he found his path blocked.

"Would you have dinner with me?"

Well, goddamn. He looked sincere. Tarek wanted to say no and leave Portland twice as intrigued. He didn't have the strength. Still, he didn't answer right away. He simply eyed Portland as if his earlier attempt to buy him had made Tarek second guess himself.

"I don't know. What's your name?"

A smile touched Portland's lips. He bit his bottom lip as if trying to stop the gesture. Tarek's heart beat a little faster. *Fuck*. He was in trouble.

"It's Portland. What's yours?"

Tarek held out his hand for Portland to shake. "I'm Tarek. It's very nice to meet you."

Portland shifted a leather bag he carried from one hand to the other and shook his hand. "You, as well."

Tarek blew out a sigh. "Well, you have a sincere handshake, so yes. I'd love to have dinner with you."

The sweetness in his expression slipped. Tarek glimpsed the hunger underneath. His skin tingled. He wouldn't have decided on Portland if he wasn't truly interested. Tarek didn't have what it took to find a ninety-year-old man with one foot in the grave and rock his world. There had to be some attraction.

Portland turned slightly and held his elbow out for Tarek like a gentleman. "I know just the place."

Tarek accepted his arm and hoped he hadn't made a fatal misstep. "You've got my curiosity up."

Portland headed toward the valet station. "My guess is, since you work here, you're likely sick of every onsite restaurant."

God, he wasn't lying. "So tired."

Portland laughed. It was sexy enough to make Tarek's breath catch. Portland handed off his ticket before sweeping Tarek outside.

A thought hit Tarek as they waited for Portland's car. "Speaking of work, I'm still wearing my dealer's uniform. Should I run home and change?"

"I can take you home first if you'd like."
His gaze swept down Tarek's body. "But
I like you just fine how you are."

Tarek swallowed. This wasn't going at all
how he expected. He was the one being
seduced. A Phantom rolled to a stop at
the curb. As Portland opened the passenger side door of the more than half a
million-dollar car, Tarek questioned his
every life choice. He chewed his bottom lip as he stepped from the curb and
climbed into the passenger seat. There
was nothing stopping Portland from mur-
dering him now. He should have taken
the stack of cash and called it a day.
His roommate had been trying to teach
him how to become a sugar baby, but he
hadn't given any lessons on how not to
end up in a shallow grave.

Portland kneeled and set his leather bag on the ground. He buckled Tarek's seatbelt for him. "Don't look so scared. I promise this is just dinner. You'll make it home safe."

Tarek forced a smile to his lips. "Sorry. This is my first time accepting an impromptu date like this."

Portland cocked his head to one side and studied Tarek. "I find that hard to believe. You're stunning. But what made you decide to accept this one?"

"I'll let you know when I figure it out."

With a laugh, Portland grabbed his bag, stood, and closed the door. Tarek took a calming breath. He could and would do this. No way in hell would Tarek spend the rest of his life crashing with his best friend and hoping for the best. Tarek might not have much, but he had looks. He had to use the commodities life handed him. Portland Wales was as good as his.

A dark cloud hung over Portland, setting his teeth on edge. He opened the trunk and stashed the bag of cash he had collected earlier in the night. Over the years, Portland had gotten very adept at hiding behind a congenial smile. Tonight, he had honestly believed, would be the night the world saw behind his mask. Portland wasn't as sure now.

The valet waited at his open driver's side door. Portland quietly slipped him a tip before climbing behind the wheel. The man closed the door, leaving him alone with his new friend. While Portland had been busy stashing his latest collection, Tarek had been busy as well. In Portland's absence, he had flipped down the sun visor and fluffed his hair into a sexy mess. Portland watched as he swiped some tinted lip balm across his lips. He dropped the tube in his bag before going to work, rolling up the long sleeves of his dress shirt to his elbows. Portland could have started their drive to the restaurant, but he was too mesmerized. There was a tattoo that began just above Tarek's wrist. It was a forest scene that encircled his arm, going halfway to his elbow.

Tarek turned his head and flashed Portland a smile. His eyes were now highlighted by dark eyeliner. In a span of five minutes, Tarek had gone from clean-cut twink to a sexy bad boy. It was almost as if Tarek intentionally showed his true self to test Portland. Portland had invited the clean version of him to dinner. This was obviously the real him. If anything, Portland was twice as turned on now.

"Are you ready? I'd hate to drive off and mess up your makeup."

A bright smile lit Tarek's face and flashed in his eyes. "Yes. Sorry. I just needed a quick refresh. You don't want to be seen with a guy in his work clothes."

Portland looked away and put the car in gear. He pulled away from the curb. "I've never cared what anyone else thinks, but I'd be proud to be seen with either version of you."

"Good. You're a gorgeous guy. I wouldn't want to embarrass you."

The clouds parted. A weight lifted from Portland's chest. He had started the night ready to ruin lives and leave bodies in his wake. The man he'd desired and chased for literally years had married someone else. Portland had been completely unprepared for the news when it had dropped less than an hour ago. When Portland had first spotted Tarek, his plan had been to punish him for Court's sins. Court was—or had been—a high-priced escort that had entertained Portland many nights. Portland had been slowly cornering Court into being completely dependent on him before Court had slipped through his fingers. His gaze slid Tarek's way when he stopped at a red light. The light from a nearby streetlamp highlighted his perfect skin. Portland inspected him on the sly. He was flawless. Portland needed to know more. It was possible Tarek could be the exact replacement Portland needed. He didn't believe in love. Portland believed in power and total control. He didn't want a partner. Portland wanted a slave, on his knees and completely beholden to him. Anyone less wouldn't tolerate his secrets.

The light turned green. Portland nearly snarled at the interruption. He needed to thoroughly research his new acquisition. Portland forced himself to be patient. He still had to learn more.

"I hope you like Greek."

A quiet laugh caressed his ears. "I actually love Greek. My mom is from Greece originally. That's basically what our daily menu consisted of growing up."

"Interesting." Tarek had opened a door. The closeness of his family mattered. A tight-knit family was a place to run home. Portland couldn't have that. "Are you close with your family?"

"Mhmm." The humming sound made Portland smile for real. Tarek chuckled. "I'm not sure where to start with that one."

"If you'd rather not talk about it, it's fine." It wasn't. "I'll understand." He wouldn't. "I'm only trying to get to know you." That much was true.

Tarek made a dismissive motion. "No. It's fine. They currently live in Biloxi, Mississippi. I don't see them often. When I turned twenty-one, I got a job at a casino. Nothing pays well there, except the shipping yard or the casinos. Obviously, I'm not built for the shipping yard, but they were not pleased. Good Catholic boys don't do all that." Tarek laughed. He did that a lot and Portland enjoyed the sound.

"Now you're in Atlantic City. I can't imagine that went over well."

Tarek made another humming sound. "It probably wouldn't if they had any idea where I am."

Portland's hopes raised. "I sense a story."

From the corner of his eye, Portland saw Tarek's hands rise and fall. "Are you sure you want to hear all this? I'm not sure this is first date material. Surely this is a three months in and surprise. I have no family."

Despite himself, a genuine laugh escaped Portland. Tarek had a way of saying things that made his confessions sound humorous rather than traumatic. "I'm a lot older than you. We move faster at my age." A thought hit him. He fully intended to have Tarek investigated, but he still liked the idea of asking all the questions. "Speaking of which, how old are you?"

"Twenty-six. How old are you?"

"Forty-seven."

A bark of laughter burst from Tarek. "You said that so darkly, as if you expected me to leap from the moving car. Forty-seven isn't old."

"Not that I remember much about being in my twenties, but I'm fairly certain I thought forty anything was old at that age. But I pulled you off topic. What happened with your parents?" He wanted that info.

A loud, dramatic-sounding and obviously fake sigh rang out from Tarek's side of the car. "If you're sure?"

Portland couldn't stop smiling, for real, and that never happened to him. "I'm sure."

"Okay. Hmmm. Where did I leave off? Oh, I went to work at a casino. So, they tried to make me quit, but I was an adult, and I was determined to save enough money to get my own place. When that didn't work, they began charging me outrageous rent, saying if I quit, then I could go back to living there for free. So I moved out with a friend from work. Obviously, my parents hated him, but there was nothing they could do. That didn't mean they gave up. My mom started showing up during my shifts with her rosary beads and praying for my soul every night, trying to get me fired. Finally, my roommate—Salem—got offered a job at the greyhound track in Pensacola. He finagled me a job too at their poker tables. So we were off and my parents were furious. Unfortunately—"

"Pensacola is only an hour and a half away," Portland said, interrupting him.

"Exactly," Tarek said with a sigh. "And things got way worse when they kept making the drive, only to be told they weren't allowed inside without a membership."

A bark of laughter burst from Portland.

"Oh, if only it had been funny longer than five minutes," Tarek said, sounding like he was really getting into the story. Portland was too. He hung on every word. "Since security wouldn't let them through the gate. Oh, side note, they didn't need a membership. I just had them banned."

Portland laughed again.

Tarek was a natural born storyteller. "Anyhow, they came up with a new plan. They started picketing the building."

Portland swiped his hand across his eyes. "Jesus." He couldn't even imagine having such ridiculous parents.

"Yep. Thankfully, though, Salem is stupidly beautiful. Within like three weeks, he had marriage offers coming out of his ass and he—"

"Wait," Portland said, cutting him off. "You're not talking about Salem Rochester, are you?"

Tarek groaned. "Don't tell me you're in love with him too."

Portland shook his head. He couldn't believe how small the world was... or his luck. Salem was a notorious gold digger. He had made a huge splash in the community by marrying a ninety-year-old billionaire with no living family other than two stepsons from two different marriages that he loved like his own. The guy had died less than a year later, leaving everything to the three. Rumor was, all three still lived in the guy's mansion because none of them were willing to concede to the others. If Tarek was friends with Salem, it was possible this was all about money. That was something he could work with.

"No. I'm not in love with him. I don't think I've ever even seen him, but I know his story, of course. I take it you came here with Salem when he was scooped up by his half dead sugar daddy."

Tarek didn't respond right away. A heavy silence fell inside the car. Finally, Tarek spoke. His voice was soft and a little sad. "Salem is my best friend, but I'm not like him. I came to Atlantic City and found a legitimate job. If I quit right now, Salem would take care of me. He can more than afford it. But I don't want to be that guy and I hope you don't think I accepted this date for any reason other than I wanted to."

He confused the hell out of Portland. Maybe Portland confused himself. Portland had money. He had come from money and did everything he could to make more. He preferred buying people over building connections. Loyalty had its price. Everything did. But—for the first time—he oddly liked the idea of Tarek being there because he wanted to be there. Despite his initial offer of money at the casino and the obvious value of his car, Portland couldn't imagine Tarek knew much—if anything—about Portland's wealth. Old money moved in silence... and drug lords moved even quieter.

Portland wanted this guy. He had to play this perfectly. "I approached you with a stack of cash. Surely you don't think I'm the type to wonder why anyone is in my life?" He chose to show part of the real him in hopes of drawing Tarek in. "When you reach a certain level of wealth, everything is for sale. You don't settle for anything in life because you don't have to. Everything and everyone has a price tag. Whether they admit it or even realize it, they're for sale. Ask your friend. JD Rochester knew your friend only wanted his money. He didn't care because he wanted a young beauty on his arm. My circles are a different breed. Most of us have no hearts."

"Was that a warning?"

Portland hated the change to Tarek. He wanted the happy, chattering, and laughing Tarek back. Portland forced his voice to lighten. "Not at all. Sorry. I was trying—obviously badly—to say I know how to spot a calculating gold digger from a mile away. I don't see that in you. You don't strike me as someone who could climb into bed with a ninety-year-old man and pretend to like it." That much he knew to be true. Tarek was too open. His feelings showed in his eyes.

Tarek chuckled softly. "That's definitely true." A louder laugh burst from Tarek. "But don't get me wrong, I can't say I don't wish I could be that person. Salem is kicked back in the lap of luxury now, without a care in the world, thanks to his charms."

Portland scoffed as he parked outside his favorite restaurant. "Who doesn't wish they had those acting abilities? JD had billions with the big B. Who wouldn't try their damnedest not to cringe and take it?"

They looked each other's way. Portland couldn't say what happened. It was as if they were two teenagers trying to stay quiet in class after sharing a private joke. Their gazes met, and they exploded into laughter. Portland tried stifling the sound, only to laugh harder. He didn't know what it was about Tarek, but Portland was already obsessed. The idea of Court vanished. Tarek was so much better.

CHAPTER TWO

THE WORLD DISAPPEARED AROUND Tarek. He stared at the ceiling from his spot on the couch and went over every detail of his date with Portland in his mind. Things hadn't gone at all like he planned. Somehow, Tarek had gone from hunting Portland to swearing he wasn't a gold digger like Salem. Fuck his life. He didn't know what happened. As soon as Portland recognized Salem's name, an overwhelming urge to ensure Portland knew he wasn't like him had overcome him. Now Tarek didn't know what he believed.

A very unclothed and tall male swept past the couch. Tarek enjoyed the show. For all Dodge's lack of intelligence, he was still one of God's favorites. It was too bad he was straight.

"I know I'll regret asking this. Why are you nude?"

Dodge looked down at his body. An empty-headed chuckle escaped him. "Oh. Yeah. I don't know."

Thank god he was pretty.

Dodge grabbed a drink from the kitchen and returned. He grabbed Tarek's feet and sat where they had been. Bare assed. On the couch. He massaged Tarek's feet, so Tarek didn't balk. Plus, it wasn't his couch. Nothing belonged to him.

"Why aren't you at work?"

Tarek stuffed a throw pillow beneath his head so he could hold Dodge's stare while they talked. He was painfully aware of exactly how far his feet were from Dodge's massive dick. "I'm off today."

"Cool. We should get high."

Tarek fought not to roll his eyes. "You know they randomly drug test at my job. I can't afford to be unemployed."

Dodge blinked at him—like the concept of money eluded him. "Sure you can. Quest and I would take care of you."

Tarek's smile was out of his control. Dodge was sweet. Tarek knew if he needed them, Dodge and Quest would have his back. Salem would snap his fingers and they would do anything to keep him happy. It was almost funny. The step-brothers were straight, but they adored Salem. People thought the three shared the mansion JD left to them because none of them were willing to let go of their portion. Nothing could be further from the truth. The three were insepara-ble. From the day JD brought Salem to live with him and his sons, it was like the three of them met their soulmates. Some-times Tarek felt like an outsider. That was why he needed to forge a new path. No matter what they claimed, Tarek was an interloper here.

"You're sweet."

Salem's head appeared over the couch. He kissed Dodge's cheek. "Hello, sweet angel. Where are your clothes?"

The same clueless chuckle Tarek had gotten fell from Dodge's lips. This time, it was accompanied by a blush. He grabbed a throw pillow and covered his crotch. "I forgot them."

Tarek and Salem exchanged a glance. Salem rolled his eyes, but he still affectionately ran his fingers down the back of Dodge's neck—like stroking a pet. "Go find them and I'll make you breakfast."

Dodge nodded. His blush didn't recede.

Tarek was fascinated.

Salem headed for the kitchen while Tarek stared at Dodge.

Dodge didn't move. For a moment, he seemed to disappear inside himself before focusing on Tarek once more. "I don't remember what we were talking about."

Tarek smiled. "That's okay. Salem's cooking will do that to a person."

The way Dodge smiled nearly made Tarek sigh. Yeah. God had favorites. Dodge stood and tossed the pillow aside. He turned away before Tarek got the full show. Tarek kind of wished he hadn't. For a moment, he almost swore Dodge was semi hard. He had zero interest in Dodge beyond friendship and the enjoyment he got from looking at the guy. Still, he would have paid good money for that show. It had been way too long since Tarek had sex. He had never been one to enjoy casual flings. Maybe he just had bad taste or something, but he had never gotten to enjoy a one-night stand that hadn't been all about getting used with zero thought to his pleasure. Tarek wouldn't waste precious prep time on that bullshit. He was done with settling.

For a full five minutes, Portland sat in his car and stared at the three-story stucco beach house. It sat on a corner lot and had its own lighthouse. While Portland had heard the stories of the mansion JD had left behind, Portland hadn't realized this was the one. He loved it, except now he truly couldn't picture Tarek being interested in his money. Why would he need Portland if he lived here? His mind had glitched a bit since pulling into the driveway. The more he learned about

Tarek, the more it looked like the guy actually wanted Portland for Portland. He didn't know how to feel.

Giving up the puzzle for now, Portland climbed from the car and headed for the door. Every new detail of the house he saw made him fall a little more in envy. The front door was unlike anything he had ever seen. It was mostly glass but solid and intricate-looking—like it was an indestructible beauty. He rang the doorbell. A musical chime floated through the air, caressing his ears. Fuck. Everything about the place was magical. The door swung open and a tiny blond sprite stared out at him. Portland knew immediately it was Salem.

Salem's sparkling green gaze slid down Portland's body before meeting his stare. He looked young. Uncomfortably young.

Portland knew he had to be old enough to get married and work at a casino a few years ago, so he had to be at least Tarek's age, if not a little older. He looked fifteen. Portland didn't find that attractive in the least.

"Is Tarek home?" Portland asked when his brain worked again.

"Portland, right?"

That threw Portland every bit as much as the sight of the house. Did Salem recognize him from somewhere, or had Tarek talked about him? Fuck. What was this feeling in his chest? He was acting like a goddamn teen with his first crush. "Yeah. You must be Salem."

An irresistible smile snapped to Salem's lips. "That's me. Come on." He waved for Portland to follow.

Portland stepped inside and closed the door behind him. "This is a beautiful house."

Before Salem responded, a half nude man who looked like a Greek god appeared at the bottom of the steps.

Salem snapped his fingers. "A shirt too, beautiful."

Looking pouty, the guy headed back up the steps.

Portland didn't ask, but he was dying with curiosity. Then it hit him. Tarek lived here with these young, beautiful men. Jealousy wormed its way through his gut, darkening his mood. He felt his features hardening with every step.

"Hey, babe. Portland is here."

For half a second, Portland was confused as to why Salem spoke to an empty room. Then Tarek shot upright from a couch that had its back to the doorway. His hair was a mess. Portland didn't see anything but his beautiful smile. It was real.

"Hey. How did you know where I live?"

Since he had dropped Tarek off at his car at the casino last night, that was a fair question. "I know everyone in this town."

Two men rushed into the room like over enthusiastic, giant puppies and nearly plowed Salem over. One was blond, and the other was the same dark-haired god from the stairs. They were equally flaw-less—like gym bros, but nice. Honestly, they both looked too dumb to be mean.

"I heard there was breakfast."

Salem chuckled and shook his head.

"Almost everyone in this town," Portland said absently as he eyed the pair. His gaze returned to Tarek. Tarek looked slightly crestfallen, as if he was used to fading into the background once the beauty brigade arrived. None of them held a candle to Tarek. Each of them had something Portland couldn't stomach. He had no desire to date someone who looked like a child, and he definitely didn't want to spend his time with someone with nothing but air in their head. Not only was Tarek gorgeous, but he was smart and funny. Witty. Everyone else disappeared.

"I've come to steal you away for the day."

The light returned to Tarek's eyes. "How did you know I'm off today? Is this another knowing everyone thing?"

"You're off today? Perfect."

Tarek laughed. It was a real one. He didn't try to look pretty. It was obvious he didn't put on an act for anyone. Tarek was his genuine self and Portland was mystified. He stood and circled the couch. "Come on." Tarek took his hand and headed for the stairs.

Portland allowed himself to get dragged along. Truthfully, it was more like he was trapped in a spell and his body obeyed. He watched the way Tarek's body moved as he climbed the steps ahead of him. Portland wanted him; almost painfully so. As they reached the second floor, Tarek kept going to the third. He spoke over his shoulder as he went. "I'm the only one whose bedroom is on the third floor. No one else likes climbing this many stairs, but I love the view." As they cleared the last step, Portland nearly gasped. The top floor was nothing but windows, and the bedroom faced the ocean.

"This house is beautiful. It's no wonder JD's stepsons refused to give it up to Salem." Portland wanted to bite his tongue off as soon as the words left his mouth. Salem was Tarek's best friend. He likely didn't care for Portland insinuating Salem shouldn't have inherited the place.

Tarek shocked him by laughing. His eyes swam with good humor. "What? Those two downstairs? They don't leave here because they're glued to Salem's hips like they were born conjoined triplets. Those three are inseparable. It's like they were born to find each other."

That confused Portland more than a little. "I'd always heard the stepsons were straight." Much to the chagrin of the entire gay community. They loved adding names to the Atlantic City's Most Wanted list of bachelors.

Tarek motioned toward his unmade bed. "Sit. They are. Friends can be soulmates too."

Portland would have to mull that one over. He was a good ninety-five percent certain friendship wasn't what he had seen downstairs. Maybe his ability to read people was fading.

Tarek peeled off his shirt. "Where are we going? I don't know how to dress."

The hunger that slammed into Portland bordered on unnatural. "What's wrong with what you're wearing?" There was a hint of a growl in Portland's voice. It was out of his control.

Tarek eyed the shirt he held. "I didn't think you'd want to be seen with me in an old band t-shirt."

Goddamn. His skin was flawless. "I just really need you to put your shirt back on." Portland wasn't doing a good job of hiding the monster inside him. "I'm sitting on your bed. You're too beautiful and it's been a really long time since anyone touched me." And he was within striking distance. All Portland had to do was pull him into bed.

Tarek didn't put his shirt back on. He stared at Portland like a deer in the head lights. His tongue shot out, wetting his bottom lip. "You haven't even kissed me yet. For all you know, I might not be that desirable."

If this was a game, Tarek was winning. All Portland heard was his pulse thumping in his ears. His skin itched. Tarek was in danger.

Showing an obvious lack of good sense, Tarek tossed his shirt aside and crowded Portland's space. He set his hands on Portland's shoulders and stared down at him, looking every bit as starved as Portland felt.

Portland's hands ran up the backs of Tarek's thighs. He didn't even realize it until he cupped Tarek's ass. It was too late for him. Portland pulled Tarek closer until Tarek straddled his lap. His breathing turned ragged. The suspense snapped Portland's razor-thin human veneer. He grabbed the back of Tarek's head and hauled him down so he could claim his mouth. Tarek didn't kiss the way Portland was accustomed. It wasn't rough and hungry. His kiss was soft and seeking. It pissed Portland off because he didn't want to be soft.

Portland flipped, pinning Tarek beneath him. He took the kiss he wanted. Tarek's knees lifted and gently brushed his sides. He held Portland's face and Portland found himself being the one who turned gentle. Tarek wasn't the type of guy a person manhandled. He was precious. Tarek looked soft—like he might bruise easily. The idea of anyone marking Tarek's skin outraged Portland. He deserved someone who took their time and blew his mind. Portland wanted to watch him fly apart. He needed that image in his head to be real.

Portland pulled away and stared down at Tarek. Possessiveness overcame him. He felt murderous at the idea of anyone coming between them. "What are you doing to me?"

Tarek chuckled. "I think it's a bit obvious."

"No. What are you doing to my head and chest?"

Tarek's smile fell. His gaze moved over Portland's face. He looked nervous. "Whatever it is, you don't look like you like it."

"People don't matter to me."

Tarek flinched as if Portland's words physically slapped him.

Portland had to fix it. "You matter to me."

"You matter to me too."

That was dumb. Portland would eat him alive.

Tarek suddenly looked uncomfortable. His gaze slid away. "No one's touched me in a long time either."

"What? Why?" Portland didn't mean to sound so disbelieving, bordering on accusatory, but he didn't understand.

Tarek met his stare again, looking defiant. "I don't do one-night stands and that's all anyone wants anymore. Either someone wants to be with me, or they don't. I don't play games."

He couldn't have been more perfect for Portland if Portland had created him from a spell. "Then I should probably go on the record and say I'm looking for more with you than one night or just sex. I just lost years of my life hopelessly trying to win someone I chose to be unexclusive with. I knew seeing me would ruin his career, and I knew how much his job meant to him. In the end, what really happened was he waited until he found someone else and then quit. I don't want to waste more time on something fake. I need something real."

Tarek held Portland's head and scratched the spot at his hairline. Goosebumps rose and Portland's skin. His desire skyrocketed. "It's probably a good thing we're searching for the same thing, since I'm not entirely sure we're leaving this bed."

Despite his erection and the painful need to seal this deal, Portland laughed. "Let me take you to breakfast first." His smile slipped. Portland showed his hunger at full force. "Plus, there's no one at my place to hear you scream."

"I'll hold you to that boast."

Portland couldn't resist the heat in Tarek's eyes. He stole another kiss. This time, he lingered, letting Tarek know through his actions that he enjoyed using his tongue. Soon enough, he would have everything he wanted. Portland felt the springs of his trap tightening.

CHAPTER THREE

IF PORTLAND HAD SAID he intended to take Tarek to breakfast at his country club, he likely would have panicked and stressed over what to wear. Since Portland wore a long sleeve t-shirt and jeans, Tarek matched his style. Thankfully, other than the staff, everyone was dressed in various states of casual. Tarek noticed the way eyes subtly moved Portland's way, checking him out on the sly. He was an extremely attractive man who looked expensive even when dressed down. It was the way he carried himself and the combination of light blue eyes and salt and pepper hair. He looked un-touchable—like a man out of everyone's league. Tarek was ridiculously proud to be seen with him. He still couldn't believe Portland wanted something serious. Tarek had fully expected to pull out all the stops to win him. It turned out that wasn't the issue. The problem was how badly Tarek wanted this to be real. He didn't think he was supposed to lose his heart in this exchange. Salem had never specified.

Tarek stared at the menu with barely ten items while Portland watched. He felt Portland's eyes upon him like a physical touch. Tarek didn't want to set the menu aside and hold a staring contest. He liked the idea of Portland studying him... letting his hunger grow. Tarek's need grew right alongside him.

"I get the feeling you either don't like breakfast foods or you're avoiding me."

With a chuckle, Tarek set the menu aside. "I'm definitely not avoiding you."

Portland's eyebrows rose. "It's not too late to go somewhere else. We can get lunch instead."

Tarek shook his head. "It's fine. I don't usually eat breakfast, but I'm good with something light, like the fruit and yogurt."

"Breakfast is the most important meal of the day."

A smile snapped to Tarek's lips. "You sounded like such a dad right then. I never thought to ask if you have any children."

The look of disgust that immediately followed his question had Tarek biting back laughter.

"No kids, then?"

Portland laughed. "Sorry. I didn't do a very good job of hiding my face." He pulled another face—this time one of child-like guilt—that had Tarek laughing. It was the most playful Tarek had ever seen him. He liked it.

"Happiness looks good on you."

At Tarek's observation, Portland's expression shifted for a moment, becoming something Tarek didn't understand before Portland immediately hid behind his usual smile. "I—"

"Portland. Hey."

Portland turned his head at the interruption.

Tarek did too.

The most beautiful man Tarek had ever set eyes on headed their way. That said a lot, considering he lived with Salem. A face Tarek had seen several times at his tables trailed behind the beauty.

Portland stood. "Court. Hey. How have you been?" They hugged.

Tarek's heart dropped. While he had heard the rumors about Portland recently losing his longtime escort to marriage, and he had heard the name, he had never actually seen Court. Tarek couldn't compete. That was a point driven home by the way Portland looked at Court. It was as if the world had disappeared. Tarek went back to staring at the menu.

"I'm Heath. You work at the Luna, correct?"

Without the mention of his job, Tarek wouldn't have realized the quietly spoken words were for him. He set the menu aside again and accepted Heath's outstretched hand. "Yeah. That's me. You've been to my table several times. I'm Tarek."

Heath briefly shook his hand and nodded. "I actually actively always pick your table. You're uniquely entertaining for such a serious job."

A laugh burst from Tarek. He had never heard anyone call his job serious. In a way, it was. He never forgot he worked for the mob. "I'm glad you choose me,

You never seem to take the game too seriously. I do a lot of talking people down from the ledge all night."

"Meh. It's not serious. Hey. Meet my husband." He grabbed Court's hand and pulled him mid-word from his conversation with Portland. "My husband, Court."

Despite whom he was introducing, Tarek couldn't stop smiling. Heath was obviously a giant child. Court looked used to this behavior.

"Tarek," Tarek said, dipping his chin.

Court shook his hand. "It's nice to meet you. Portland was just telling me the story of how you two met."

Tarek's gaze slid Portland's way for a moment. He refused to let his smile slip. "Was he now?" Tarek's blood boiled. He shouldn't care that Portland obviously tried to make Court jealous by using him. That was how he felt, though. Used.

"It's very sweet. I'm glad to see him so happy."

"Me too."

They exchanged a smile.

"It looks like our table is ready." Heath nodded toward a spot across the room. He focused on Tarek again. "It was good seeing you. Enjoy your breakfast."

Tarek nodded and kept smiling through the parting pleasantries. All he could think about was the way Portland looked at Court. He wasn't supposed to be jealous. Why in the fuck did he feel this way?

"It's always awkward to run into your ex."

Portland froze. "How did you..."

"It's the way you looked at him. It was pretty obvious."

Portland winced. "Sorry about that. Truthfully, he isn't technically my ex. We were never much more than me fruitlessly chasing him."

Tarek glanced toward the table where Court sat. "I can see why. He's incredibly beautiful."

"That's not why I chased him."

That brought Tarek's gaze back to Portland. Portland looked so dark and serious; Tarek had to know. "Why?" As soon as he asked, Tarek felt dumb. The guy was obviously amazing in other ways than looks. Of course, Portland would chase him.

But Portland shocked him. "Because I knew I could own him. I knew the difference in our financial situations left him vulnerable to me, and he would be loyal if I forced his hand."

Tarek wasn't dumb. He saw Portland and heard all the warning bells. Tarek didn't know if it was the thrill of danger or his need to win, but he was completely on board. "Do you feel the same about us?" He had already told Portland he didn't like games. Tarek preferred they be up-front.

"I'm already much deeper with you than I ever was with him. That should probably scare you."

Tarek wanted to ask why Portland hadn't pushed Court beyond Court being a well-known escort who made his living dating other people. Portland could have kept Court in any lifestyle of his choosing. Tarek was afraid the answer might hurt his feelings—like Court had a world of other options Tarek didn't have.

Portland's gaze moved over Tarek's face, as if he read his mind. Then, he proved he did. "You look at me in a way he never did. I knew if I won him with money, that was all it would ever be, and that might never be enough to hold him. If you want my money, it's not all you want."

God. His pride wanted to sting a hair over getting called out for his thirst, but fuck. Portland wasn't wrong. Tarek hadn't expected this deep of an attraction, but he wasn't disappointed because he felt pretty damn sure it went both ways.

"Accepting that dinner date is starting to feel like one of the best decisions I've made."

A sexy smile slowly spread across Portland's lips. "You're really not the least bit worried about what dating me might look like, are you?"

Tarek shook his head. "There's a lot you're holding back. I see flashes of the real you here and there. I'm just waiting for that guy to appear on full display because I'm pretty sure I'll love every second of it."

Portland sat back in his chair, looking thoughtful. His gaze never wavered from Tarek. Tarek refused to look away. He wanted this. Being owned sounded a hell of a lot better than being loved. Love had driven him all the way to Atlantic City when the people who were supposed to love him the most proved it came with terms and conditions.

"Where is our fucking server? I'm ready to take you to bed."

Tarek bit his bottom lip, fighting a sassy smile. Portland would be absolute fire in bed. Tarek couldn't wait to see firsthand.

The hurt that had crossed Tarek's features when he obviously realized who Court was still hurt Portland's chest. He shouldn't care. Portland had no idea why he did, but that pain meant jealousy. Goddamn. It felt amazing to be wanted.

Not just sought after for his money and status, but fucking desired. Portland had thought he didn't care about that bullshit, but goddamn. He wanted this. Tarek either wasn't good at hiding his thoughts or he didn't care who saw them. Portland didn't have to guess at his intentions. Their attraction went both ways.

Breakfast had gone painfully slow. From the moment Court walked away and forced their discussion, Portland had forgotten anyone else existed. He had never been so close to screaming in frustration in his life. The drive to his place wasn't much better. Traffic was lighter than usual and still nothing moved quickly enough. Tarek held his hand. He played with Portland's fingers—like Portland wouldn't destroy him if he betrayed him.

The gate to his property slid open as Portland approached. He didn't imagine Tarek would be impressed, considering where he lived. Still, Portland couldn't resist turning his head to check Tarek's reaction to his home. He found Tarek staring at him. The breath froze in his lungs. His dark eyes were sexy. He bled sensuality. Portland didn't know if he would make it. He was hard already from just thinking about Tarek's lithe body beneath him.

He pulled into the garage. His patience stretched thinner by the second. Tarek stepped out without waiting for him, as if he too couldn't take much more of this. Portland motioned toward the door that led to the mudroom. When Tarek reached it, Portland molded against his back. He kissed Tarek's nape, lingering when Tarek dropped his chin to his chest, giving him better access. Chill bumps rose beneath his lips, mesmerizing him and making him want more. His hands found Tarek's hips before moving up and beneath his shirt. He kept going, pushing Tarek's shirt higher until he peeled it from Tarek's body. More goosebumps rose beneath his fingertips as he dropped the shirt and skimmed his fingers down Tarek's torso. Portland's lips wouldn't budge from Tarek's skin. He smelled too perfect.

Portland popped the button on Tarek's jeans. "I've never wanted to fuck someone so badly against a door in my life."

Tarek took a ragged breath, somehow making Portland even harder. His every reaction to Portland was one hundred percent genuine. There was no way he could fake the way his body responded. Portland's head was all over the place. He craved a million things he never expected. Portland had feared himself more times than he wanted to admit. He had never been as scared as he was in that moment of how far he would go.

Portland reached past Tarek and set his finger on the fingerprint scanner, unlocking the door. "But I want you bent over my bed, biting my sheets even more."

"Oh, God."

A wicked smile pulled at Portland's lips at the words. He could show a little patience. Tarek would be worth it in the end. He urged Tarek inside and shuffled him down the hall. His gaze slid past all the rich furnishings and art he had amassed over the years, trying desperately to buy happiness. Portland's mind was in one place: inside Tarek. The bright early afternoon sun poured through his bedroom window, brightening the place more than having the lights on. Portland was good with that. He wanted to inspect every inch of the body he intended to buy, and Portland fully planned to buy Tarek. Portland would shower the guy with so many gifts, he'd never leave. That was all Portland had going for him.

He worked on divesting Tarek of his clothes as he shuffled him toward the bed. Portland kissed and bit Tarek's shoulders and neck, keeping him ready to go. Before he could bend Tarek over the bed, as promised, Tarek spun and captured his mouth. He came at Portland hot and wild while tearing at Portland's clothes. Portland lifted his arms and twisted, doing whatever move was needed for Tarek to get him nude. When Tarek's fingers encircled Portland's overly sensitive cock, Portland nearly blew.

"Please. I want it."

The neediness in Tarek's plea broke something in Portland's brain. He had missed this in his life. Every day, he felt the lack. The problem was not just anyone would do. Portland wasn't interested in subpar sex with someone as bored by life as him. He needed someone like Tarek. Someone who hadn't tried everything twice and some things a million times. He needed to taste the freshness of the moment on Tarek's innocent skin.

Portland lifted Tarek from his feet and tackled him on the bed. He wasted no time finding the lube and a condom.

Portland kissed Tarek's stomach as he lubed his asshole. His self-restraint had reached its limit. Portland wanted to do all the things that would have Tarek coming back for more. His back teeth were already on the verge of cracking from him clenching his jaw.

Tarek grabbed his chin and forced Portland to meet his stare. He spoke through clenched teeth. "Stop teasing. Inside me. Now."

Portland might have laughed if he hadn't been so aroused. Teasing? Portland felt like he had barely touched Tarek. He definitely hadn't given the guy an ounce of foreplay. What kind of men had Tarek slept with that he didn't even realize that? Still, Portland couldn't disobey. He might not last if he tried anything else. Next time, he would take his time and show Tarek exactly how much pleasure his body could bring. For now, he surged upward, captured Tarek's mouth, and shoved his way inside.

Tarek cried out.

Portland froze. He saw stars. Tarek was tight. He nearly broke Portland. He was so focused on not immediately blowing, it took him a second to realize the reason Tarek's body gripped him so tightly was because he came.

Damn. Portland stared down at him in wonder. He was the most responsive person Portland had ever seen. Tarek writhed beneath him like he couldn't get enough. The sounds he made kept Portland frozen. He had to memorize every second. Then his own needs took control, except something inside him calmed. He savored Tarek. Portland kissed him slowly and sweetly while rocking inside him. Their fingers linked as Portland made love to Tarek. He wanted Tarek to remember every second. The way Portland would relive this day a million times.

An itch began at the base of Portland's spine. His motions quickened. Tarek felt amazing on his cock. Portland didn't want to blow. Not yet. His body didn't care about his mind's desires. The spring inside him wound tighter. His breathing quickened. He pressed his forehead against Tarek's shoulder and squeezed his eyes closed.

"Fuck. You feel too good. I want to stay here all day, but you're killing me."

Tarek tensed for half a second and then came again. It was so unexpected, it pulled an orgasm from Portland.

Portland sucked air and rode the waves. He tried breathing through the powerful orgasm. Portland never would have suspected Tarek for one of those guys who only needed a light touch. He could probably use some orgasm denial, but Portland loved how easily he gave Tarek two orgasms. Now he wanted to see how many he could give the guy in one night.

"Sorry. I told you it's been a while." Tarek's teeth chattered on the apology.

Portland went from flying high to scrambling to calm Tarek.

His body shook. "Sorry," he said again. "I don't know what's happening to me."

Portland hugged him tightly, trying to keep him warm through the shock. He had never seen sub drop from such vanilla sex, but he would recognize it anywhere.

Portland kissed Tarek's cheek and gently shushed him. "It's okay. Give it a second. It'll pass. It's just your body adjusting to the sudden surge of powerful emotions. I've got you."

After a moment, the shaking subsided, and Tarek took a ragged breath. "That's never happened to me before. I'm sorry. I didn't see that coming."

Portland kissed his neck and smiled against his skin. "Stop apologizing. I obviously did my job." And he planned to do it again. Now that he knew exactly how to handle Tarek's body, Portland had no intentions of ever giving up his new toy.

CHAPTER FOUR

THE DAY PASSED WITH them lounging in bed, talking and stealing sweet kisses. It was the best day of Tarek's life. He wanted to be embarrassed by how quickly he had blown, and his panic attack afterward, but Portland's constant praise made it impossible. Tarek couldn't say he had been disappointed.

"Do you have any big dreams for yourself, or have you always had a passion for poker?"

Tarek rolled his eyes and laughed.

Portland squeezed him. "I'm serious. What do you want to be when you grow up?"

A huff burst from Tarek. "Sir, are you insinuating I'm not grown?"

"You know better. Why are you avoiding the question?"

Tarek bit his bottom lip.

Their feet brushed beneath the covers.

Portland leaned away a hair and studied Tarek's face. "You're embarrassed. Why are you embarrassed?"

Tarek shrugged. "Okay, but you can't laugh."

"I won't." His smile said otherwise, but Tarek decided to let it go.

Tarek took a deep breath. "Okay, so. When I was like thirteen four-teen—somewhere around there—I was in this DND club. I wrote all our campaigns." Despite himself, Tarek couldn't help but smile. "It was pretty impressive, if I do say so myself. Everything was perfectly organized. I had every-thing in PDF form and printed out for each session." Tarek shrugged again. He checked Portland's expression to see if he was ready to laugh yet. Portland mere-ly looked interested. Tarek kept going. "Anyhow, this led me to start writing big-ger worlds. From there, whole stories spawned. Once I had about five or six, I realized they could be enjoyed as a serial or broken up into campaigns. So, like al-ways, I had everything all organized and a single copy printed into a hardback. I still write and just kind of play with the same world, but I guess that one book is sort of my dream board in a way. That's what I want for real. I want someone to magically see my work, print them exactly like that one, and for them to end up in clubs all over the world for players to enjoy. I want people enjoying my campaigns and getting lost in my worlds. It's a stupid and impossible dream, but that's the only future I ever fantasize about. It certainly isn't poker. But a game is a game, right?" Tarek chuckled. Even he heard the discomfort in it.

"Have you ever researched how to achieve that dream?"

Heat crawled up Tarek's face. He cleared his throat. "Achieving that dream would mean people actually reading what I wrote, and that sounds terrifying. I'm a candy ass. I can't handle criticism." Another uncomfortable laugh escaped him. He couldn't stop. They needed to stop talking about him. "What about you? Did you always dream of being the CEO of the largest bank on the east coast, or do you also have a humiliating story?"

Portland didn't laugh the way he'd hoped. His humor wasn't saving him today. "It takes a lot of talent to write. I had to write a ton of essays in college. It sucked. People don't realize how hard it is to string thousands of words together in an interesting way. You should be proud."

Secretly, he was, but there was no future in his writing. "Can we talk about you? I don't need you thinking I'm a nerd."

A sexy laugh rumbled from Portland. "Baby, you have a D20 tattooed on your back."

Tarek felt his blush return. "You know what a D20 is, so there's that, I guess."

"I don't live under a rock."

Portland's smile was everything. He was so incredibly handsome, and more than Tarek expected. Tarek flattened his palm against Portland's chest and gently rolled him onto his back. He touched his lips to the corner of Portland's mouth as he straddled Portland's body. Tarek teased Portland's lips apart. Their tongues brushed before Tarek pulled away again and went back to toying with his lips. His bottom lip was the perfect amount of plump for Tarek to nibble. Portland's nipples were hard. Tarek stroked one, enjoying the way it felt beneath his fingertips. Portland's hands ran up his back. Tarek almost hissed at the way his body immediately responded. He kissed a path to Portland's ear, lightly biting his earlobe.

"I've never been this happy." Tarek wondered if the confession was a mistake. Maybe someone like Portland would want someone a little less needy. Someone who led him on a chase. Tarek couldn't help it. He felt more than he wanted.

"That's good. I plan to keep you that way."

Tarek smiled against Portland's neck as he kissed him. Portland sounded breathless. Tarek planned to keep him that way. He bit, kissed, and sucked his way down Portland's torso. The shaky way Portland breathed was music to Tarek's ears. He palmed Portland's erection and stroked.

"I'm not as young as you."

Tarek swallowed Portland's cock, putting a stop to all the nonsense. He didn't expect anything in return. Tarek had surpassed the need to blow. He needed an outlet for the fucking happiness that choked him. When Salem had named possible candidates for Tarek to seduce, Tarek had been less than enthusiastic about this adventure. He was sick of being alone, but Salem insisted he find a wealthy man. No sense in wasting his youth on love when security meant so much more, according to Salem. Tarek assumed he knew. After all, Salem was now free to enjoy whomever he pleased with no worries about his future. Tarek didn't imagine that kind of lightning struck twice. He wasn't likely to be in the same boat. So Tarek had secretly hoped for love and money. It was possible he was on his way to both. A boy had to eat.

A chuckle rumbled from Tarek at his thoughts.

Portland's fingers dove into Tarek's hair as a moan filled the air. "Fuck, Tarek. Just like that."

Tarek settled in to tease and please. He took his time. This relationship was exactly what he wanted. He needed Portland to understand it.

Sweat coated Portland's skin. He wondered if he would die like this. Tarek had sucked his dick so long and perfectly Portland thought his heart might give out. Each time he nearly came, Tarek would move away, denying him his orgasm. It was hell and heaven. Nothing existed except Tarek's mouth. Goddamn. Portland wanted to keep him.

The tension built again, winding tighter than ever before. "Please? Fuck. Please?"

Tarek chuckled around his dick.

Portland flew apart. He forgot to breathe. His lungs seized as he shook. The level of ecstasy that roared through him was unlike anything he had ever experienced, and that said a lot. He had thought there was nothing left to experience. Tarek had proved him wrong. He was beautiful in every way.

Tarek kissed his stomach.

Portland fought for air like he had run a marathon. "Give me a minute and I'll return the favor." He gasped out the words between struggling breaths.

He felt Tarek's lips shape into a smile against his skin. "You're fine. I just want to hold you." His kisses moved upward until he rested on Portland's chest with his ear pressed against him. "You have a nice heartbeat."

It was such an odd thing to say. He imagined everyone's heart sounded the same. But it was an incredibly sweet thing to say, nonetheless. The claim still made

Portland smile. "Tell me what you want. I'll buy you anything."

He felt Tarek shake with silent laughter.

"Why are you laughing? I'm being serious. You deserve a prize after that."

Tarek laughed harder.

Portland found himself smiling. He supposed he did sound ridiculous—like he tried paying off a whore. Portland's smile disappeared. "There I go again, trying to buy you. I hope you know that's not how I meant it. You deserve beautiful things because it's you. I have money. That's all. I'm not trying to bribe you or purchase favors or whatever. Fuck." He was rambling and couldn't stop. "I don't know what I'm saying, but I hope you do."

Tarek pushed his way higher and claimed Portland's lips, cutting off the spew of nonsense.

Portland's muscles relaxed. Tarek understood. He knew this was more... maybe. Goddamn it. Tarek had to know it was more. He cupped Tarek's face and held him away so he could look into his eyes. "I don't want you to see anyone else. For once, I need to be with someone who wants only me."

"Lucky you. You're the only person I want." Tarek made the claim, wearing the sweetest of smiles. It vanished. "What if I don't want you seeing anyone else either?" He visibly swallowed. "I don't think I could handle that."

Portland kissed the tip of Tarek's nose. "You definitely have nothing to worry about. Not only have I always been a one-man guy, but I've been single a long goddamn time and haven't found anyone who makes me feel the way you do."

A shy-looking smile touched Tarek's lips. "Oh. Okay."

Fuck. Sometimes he threw off such an innocent vibe. It was at such odds with the version of Tarek that had just sucked his dick. Portland had to taste the purity on Tarek's tongue. While Tarek might not be virtuous, he sure as hell wasn't anything like Portland. His chest hurt as their tongues brushed. If they did this for real, one day, Tarek would see the real him. He would find out all Portland's dirty secrets. Portland didn't know if Tarek could or would look past his faults.

Determination filled Portland's heart. He would give Tarek the world. Portland would spoil the fuck out of him, showering him with so much affection and gifts, he wouldn't be able to leave. He would trap him—like a web. Portland would make sure Tarek couldn't get away. This time, he wouldn't fail. Tarek wasn't like Court. There was a slight insecurity in him he tried to hide behind boldness. Portland saw the real him, though. He knew exactly how to play this. Tarek wouldn't get away.

CHAPTER FIVE

THE INSECURITY SET IN as soon as Tarek was out of sight. Portland made it five hours before he blew up Tarek's phone with texts. When his messages went ignored, Portland worked on grinding his back teeth to a pulp. He made it another two and a half hours before he stormed into the casino, hunting his prey. People who always only saw him at his most congenial scampered from his path the moment they saw his expression. Portland couldn't imagine how he looked. Probably like he intended to murder someone. He wasn't sure that wasn't exactly what he planned to do. Portland had told Tarek they were a couple now. If he had forgotten that already, Portland might do anything.

Finally, Tarek came into view. He stood stoically at an empty table. Some days were like that. People chose slots over cards. Portland's shoulders eased a hair. At least Tarek hadn't lied about working today. He tried to calm his temper. Honestly, he felt a little ridiculous since he had driven Tarek to work this morning. Of course, he could have left with someone else. He didn't know why he couldn't break this ugly cycle in his head. Then Tarek turned his head and their gazes met. Tarek underwent a complete transformation. He went from the professional dealer to just a man. One who was visibly elated to see his man. Portland calmed. His ego had the balm it needed. Still, he couldn't handle being ignored, and it was best for Tarek to understand that now. Portland wouldn't tolerate having his messages unanswered.

He snagged a barstool at the chest high table.

Tarek's eyes sparkled with happiness. "Hey, gorgeous."

"You've been ignoring my texts."

Tarek looked a bit confused, but quickly rallied. "I'm not allowed to look at my phone while I'm here."

Portland felt a little stupid. Of course, Tarek wouldn't be allowed to touch his phone on the floor. An uncomfortable chuckle escaped Portland. "I didn't think of that. Maybe just ignore my texts when you turn on your phone. My messages might've gotten a little unhinged by the end."

Tarek's smile never dimmed. "That's okay." He checked his watch. "I'm off in five. If I head for the office to sign out, I'll get there just in time." He grabbed the clear bag he carried for work from beneath the table. "Here." He tossed the bag to Portland. "My phone is inside. The code is five five one nine nine eight to unlock it. Just delete the messages. Then don't think about it again."

"You're amazing." The words fell from his lips, sounding as relieved as he felt. Portland had definitely shown his crazy self in those messages.

94

Tarek winked. "I'll be right back."

Portland enjoyed the show of watching him walk away for a moment before turning his attention to Tarek's phone. He switched on the device and watched his wild spiral unfold on the face of his phone. Portland quickly deleted them before snooping through Tarek's phone. There weren't any nudes. Not of Tarek or anyone else. There were no texts with other men besides his roommates. A cursory glance showed those as mundane. After a quick glance to ensure Tarek wasn't heading back, he put the phone away and checked the rest of the bag. He didn't know what he thought he might find, since it was clear per the casino's rules, but a day of being ignored had fucked with his head. A thought hit and Portland grabbed the phone again. With a few clicks, he shared Tarek's location with himself and ensured the settings gave him permanent full-time access. Portland put the device away and dug his phone from his pocket. He sent Tarek a sweet message to make up for being psycho.

Portland: *Thank you for being perfect for me. I notice everything you do.*

There. Now he didn't feel so guilty. With nothing left to do, Portland eyed the room. He saw a few faces he recognized. The casino's manager, Saul, had guards milling the floor. To most, they likely looked like customers searching for the best machine. Portland had come here too long and knew too many people.

A few more minutes passed before he spotted Tarek heading his way. Portland swore his heart beat a little faster with each step Tarek took in his direction. He skipped the last steps to Portland's side.

Portland realized he smiled like an idiot. "Hey."

Tarek beamed at him. "Hey. I really want to kiss you right now, but I'm still in uniform and on the floor. Even off the clock, I'm not sure how Saul would react."

Portland sat Tarek's bag on the table. "Come here. Let's do this." He urged Tarek closer and removed the vest portion of Tarek's uniform, along with his tie. Portland set it on top of Tarek's bag before working on rolling up the long black sleeves of his dress shirt to his elbows and undoing the top few buttons. Next, he ran his fingers through Tarek's hair, messing up the perfect professional-looking style he wore. He eyed his work. "There. You're only missing your makeup, but no one can say shit." Portland hauled Tarek forward and covered Tarek's mouth with his. He poured the entire day's worth of anxiety into the kiss, punishing Tarek for making him worry. Tarek's hands swept up his chest. His loving touch had Portland matching his energy. Their kiss turned sweet.

Portland pulled away just far enough to press his forehead against Tarek's. He didn't open his eyes. Portland simply savored the peace and whatever this feeling was in his chest. An embarrassed chuckle escaped him. "I guess I missed you a little today."

Tarek kissed the tip of his nose. "Good. I missed you too."

That was all Portland needed to hear. He slipped from the stool and grabbed Tarek's things. With Tarek's belongings in one arm, he held his hand out for Tarek. "Let's go."

Tarek didn't hesitate to link fingers with him. In fact, he also clung to the arm of the hand he held, sticking close to Portland's side. Pride swelled his chest as they walked through the casino to the valet stand. Tarek was his. He had no reason to worry.

"What did you do today after dropping me off?"

If he was a paranoid guy, he might have seen the question as a jab at not trusting Tarek. He had brought Tarek to work. It was dumb as fuck to think Tarek had ghosted him. Some of his things were literally still at Portland's place. But Tarek wasn't the type to kick a man while he was down. Allowing him to delete those texts proved that.

"I went to the office and sat through several boring meetings and conference calls. How was your day?"

He felt Tarek shrug. "Kind of boring, actually. The days where I stand there with zero players and no tips—like today—are the worst. Not only do I see and feel every second of the day ticking by, I don't make much money. It's kind of depressing." An odd look crossed Tarek's features. "Forget I said any of that. I just realized how I sounded."

That confused the fuck out of Portland. "What do you mean? You sounded frustrated by the day to me. That happens to everyone."

Tarek still looked aggravated with himself. "That's how guys talk when they're hoping they'll get an offer to supplement their income."

Portland towed Tarek close and kissed his forehead. "Baby, even if you were doing that, I'm unbothered. It never crossed my mind you were gearing up to ask for money, but you'll also never have to ask. You'll never go without." He turned away to deal with the valet before Tarek could argue. Portland didn't want to hear it. Tarek was his, and Portland wouldn't be accused of neglecting him in any fashion. His sexy baby didn't need this job. Portland was just biding his time before he forced him to quit.

Tarek couldn't understand why getting what he sought from the very beginning felt so wrong. Hearing Portland openly talk about supporting him made Tarek question himself. His pride pricked. He hadn't expected that. Tarek realized he should have, since he had always been deeply independent. But it wasn't that. He watched Portland interact with the valet. The way his smile went from polite to steamy as it turned from the guy fetching his car to Tarek. Tarek's heart skipped a beat. His breath caught. He felt something. Fuck. Tarek wanted this for real. This had never truly been about money. He had watched Portland and plotted, but somewhere along the line, he had become obsessed.

Tarek pressed his hand against his stomach as it fluttered. He couldn't breathe.

Portland's smile disappeared. A line appeared between his eyebrows. "What's wrong? Are you feeling okay?"

Tarek didn't think. He simply snagged a handful of Portland's shirt and hauled him forward. He kissed Portland like he planned to fuck him because he did. Tarek didn't care who saw. This was real. It was really real. Overwhelmed didn't begin to cover the way he felt. He pulled away but melted into Portland's arms, snuggling against his chest.

A sexy rumble of soft laughter brushed his ear. "What was that all about?"

Tarek kissed Portland's neck. "It just hit me how grateful I am to have found you. I didn't expect you, but I'm..." Tarek blew out a breath. "I don't know what I'm trying to say. You're making me feel things."

Portland's arms tightened around him. His lips brushed the shell of Tarek's ear. "Same."

Tarek pulled away. The longer they stood there, the longer it would take them to get home. His brow furrowed as he spotted the valet still standing where Portland left him. "Is there a reason that guy isn't getting your car?"

Portland glanced over his shoulder.

"Saul would like to speak with you both in his office."

Tarek's heart dropped at the arrival of Saul's guard. Mac was one of Saul's personal guards—like one who took care of problems. With the mob, that made him fucking terrifying. The way Portland's face hardened, transforming him into a stranger, made Tarek realize Portland knew it too.

"I take it this isn't really a request."

At Portland's question, a terrifying smile touched Mac's lips. "Not really, no."

Portland dipped his chin. "Very well." He set his palm on the small of Tarek's back and motioned with the arm that still had Tarek's things draped over it. "Lead the way."

Mac's smile turned even more feral. "You know the way. I think I'll follow."

As scared as Tarek was, he also experienced several odd thoughts. Mac seemed to be focused more on Portland than him. They seemed to know each other. Mac didn't appear to trust Portland, and strangest of all, he got the feeling Mac thought Portland was dangerous—like he had to watch his back. Tarek was confused as hell.

As they crossed the threshold into Saul's office, Tarek clasped his hands to keep them from shaking. He didn't want to lose this job. Tarek didn't understand what he had done wrong. Saul met his stare first. A kind smile touched his lips. Unfortunately, Saul possessed the most terrifying eyes Tarek had ever seen, so the smile didn't really help. His eyes were a light gray that cut through a person. Tarek might have questioned if he had a soul, but he had seen the guy with his husband. There was a human in there. But then Saul's eyes slid Portland's way, and all warmth died. If Saul had been looking at him, Tarek might've taken a step back. His anxiety skyrocketed.

"Have a seat."

Tarek sat.

Portland argued. "What is all this about, Gabris? We were headed home." His voice didn't even sound like Portland. Tarek couldn't stop looking between Saul and him. Their cold stare-down was eerie. He felt like he started a movie halfway through and missed the entire plot.

Saul looked away, dismissing him. When he focused on Tarek, he turned human again. "How are you doing tonight?"

Tarek didn't know how to answer. He went with honesty. "I suppose that depends on the nature of this conversation."

Saul chuckled. "It's fine. We just have a small problem that can be easily resolved." He motioned Portland's way without looking at him. "Mr. Wales is a regular high roller at this establishment. This puts us in an awkward position."

Tarek's heart sank. He hadn't even considered that. He should have. Tarek knew how closely everything was watched. The casino would never risk there being any chance of odds leaning away from the house. "I see."

"I don't," Portland grumbled. "I spend a lot of fucking money here."

Saul's friendly smile turned feral. When he spoke, his voice sounded like it came between clenched teeth, and he didn't look Portland's way. "And we'll accept it no matter how it's earned."

Tarek found that odd. In fact, this entire situation felt a little fucked. He had to turn down the heat. "What do you need from me? I don't want to lose my place in high roller." He had worked too fucking hard to get bumped from the highest tipping job at the casino.

"You're fine." His gaze moved to Portland. "I just ask that Mr. Wales choose a different dealer when he visits us." He focused on Tarek again. "And any public displays be off the clock, off the floor, and out of uniform."

Tarek nodded. "Sounds fair."

"No."

Tarek's head snapped around at Portland's growled response. His face was hard enough to cut glass and Tarek nearly gasped. Portland was more than a little scary. Still, Tarek needed Portland to stop. This was his job on the line. He touched Portland's arm. "It's okay. I don't think it's unreasonable—"

"No," Portland repeated, cutting him off. He didn't look Tarek's way. His murderous stare never wavered from Saul's. Saul's guards subtly moved closer. Portland either didn't notice or didn't care. "Tarek has done nothing to deserve your suspicions. He's good at his job and loyal to this place. You won't disrespect him by treating him like a cheat, and I'll sit wherever the fuck I like."

Saul was every bit as scary. "My problem isn't with Tarek. I know he's a good person. You seem to forget I know you, though, and this is my casino. You're on my fucking turf. I choose who stays and where they fucking sit."

"Whose turf?" Portland said, obviously mocking him.

Saul snorted. "If you'd like to take it up with someone else, feel free. I'm not sure you'd enjoy that outcome. There's money and then there's *money*. One lackey versus an entire block of establishments. Don't overvalue yourself and end up..." Saul smiled as he trailed off, leaving his threat unsaid. "What'll it be?"

"That's a shame." Portland held his hand out to Tarek. Tarek didn't hesitate to take it. "As much as I'm sure you won't notice, you've lost this high roller and your customers' favorite dealer."

"Wait. What?" Tarek was confused as hell.

Saul's expression snapped closed. He focused on Tarek. "Say the word. If you're not safe, don't leave this office. We can keep him from taking you."

"What?" Tarek had no clue why he kept repeating that single question, but it was all he could get out between Saul and Portland arguing.

"I dare you to try, Gabris."

Saul stood and his guards closed in, forming a tight circle. They wouldn't be leaving.

Tarek panicked. "It's okay. For God's sake. Everyone stand down. I don't know what in the hell is happening here, but just stop." He had to defuse this. No matter the cost. The alternative meant their lives. "Please. I swear I'm safe. There's no reason for all this." He held Portland's arm in a tight hug. "Let's just go home like we planned. This is out of control for no reason. I'm starved and my head is pounding."

At his final statement, Portland's gaze snapped his way. His features softened, turning concerned. "Why didn't you say anything?" He kissed Tarek's forehead. "I'm sorry. I didn't think about you not eating yet today."

Saul looked confused. His gaze slid between them. He cleared his throat. "If you change your mind, Tarek, your job will be here. You'll always have a place here with us."

Tarek dipped his chin. Sadness washed over him. "Thank you. I've loved working here."

Saul looked as upset as Tarek felt—like he witnessed a tragedy. "Please call me if you need help."

Tarek managed a small smile. He didn't know how it looked, but it felt fake as hell. "Thank you. I will."

"He won't and doesn't need you." Portland's voice was back to being a stranger.

Tarek urged him toward the door. "Let's go, baby. I need some food."

Portland looked at him again like an overly concerned father. His gaze moved over Tarek's features. Tarek must have looked as bad as he felt because Portland nodded. "Okay, angel. I'll stop somewhere on the way home." Without another word or glance for Saul, Portland led him from the room.

Tarek fought not to look at anyone. He felt like a goddamn idiot. His chest hurt. He was confused and upset. It seemed he no longer had a job, and he wasn't even sure who was at fault because the entire situation seemed to have absolutely nothing to do with him. Tarek tried like hell to gather his thoughts as they headed back to the valet stand. In the end, only one thought repeated loudly in his mind. What in the hell had he gotten himself into?

CHAPTER SIX

THE STIFF, SHOCKED SILENCE Tarek rode home in had Portland ready to snap. Even after Portland gave him a drink and headache medicine, he stared at nothing—like a broken toy. Portland ordered them food and waited for Tarek to come back to himself. It aggravated Portland more than a little that Tarek obviously didn't believe Portland would take good care of him.

When his nerves finally broke, Portland headed for the garage. He grabbed the expensive leather duffle bag from the trunk. Portland almost laughed at the way he had forgotten about it until now, considering the lengths he had gone to collect. He stormed back inside and dumped the bag on Tarek's lap.

"Would you please stop looking like I destroyed your life? I told you I would take care of you. You don't need to work."

Tarek blinked. He glanced down at the bag. "What's this?"

"It's yours." Portland stood over him with his hands on his hips. He realized it probably looked like he tried to intimidate him and relaxed his pose and softened his tone. "Seriously, baby. I won't let anything happen to you."

Tarek unzipped the bag. His entire body froze. "Is this a bag of cash?"

Portland resisted the urge to roll his eyes. It was obviously a bag of cash. "Fifty grand. Deposit it as you need it, but never deposit more than nine grand at a time. You don't want to trigger the IRS. If you need more than nine K for something, just let me know and I'll buy it."

Tarek's chin lifted. "You've been carrying around fifty thousand dollars in your trunk all week."

Portland shrugged. "It's not like I've needed it."

Tarek blinked. "But... why? You came out of the casino with this. Did you win it?"

Portland didn't lie. He wanted to climb from as few holes as possible when Tarek learned the truth about him. "In a way. I collected on a debt."

Tarek moved the bag from his lap to the coffee table. He twisted his fingers, looking ready to cry. "Will you tell me why Saul doesn't trust you?"

Portland's shoulders relaxed. Tarek didn't sound like he intended to boot Portland to the curb. Talking was a good sign. He joined Tarek on the couch and stole one of his hands so he'd stop fidgeting. "Saul works for one of the biggest and most protected criminals in the country. He doesn't trust anyone. Trusting people could get him killed."

"I've seen him with his husband. He trusts him."

Portland smiled. "I'm sure that's different. There's not a person in his sphere that isn't fully investigated. Yes, that includes you. He knows who the innocents are in his life. Yes, that includes you. I, on the other hand, am also considered powerful in my own right. That makes me dangerous in his eyes. I can afford to challenge him in certain ways. In his world, that's a bad thing."

Tarek nodded. He relaxed and Portland pulled him against his side.

Portland pressed his lips to Tarek's temple and stayed like that for a moment. He needed to breathe in that innocence Portland spoke of for a minute. "I'll open you an account at my bank tomorrow. You'll be okay."

Tarek didn't respond. He just picked at the material on Portland's pants.

Portland broke. "I'm sorry. It's not fair you got caught in the middle. I've should've seen this coming."

Tarek flashed him a sweet but sad smile. "No. I should've considered how it would look for me to date a customer. The rules around there are pretty strict. Even though there's no actual written rule about dating players, since I'm sure they don't want to alienate smaller spenders, I should've considered they wouldn't approve of me dating a high roller."

Portland leaned his head against the couch and stared at Tarek. He was beautiful and saw the best in other people in a way Portland could never. Tarek was everything Portland wasn't. He was exactly what Portland needed. "I don't deserve you. We haven't been together long, and you've already tolerated more than you should have to from me. Would you believe me if I promised things will get better?"

Tarek's face transformed. He became his usual sweet and sassy self. Goddamn, he was resilient and obviously saw the best in everyone. "Tonight was bad, but I still can't imagine what you consider better. This past week with you has been the best week of my life. I don't know what I expected when I accepted that dinner offer. But what I found is so much better than anything I could've imagined. I honestly feel like we have something—like there's something growing here. Do you want to find out what it is? Because I do. I'm pretty sure I want it more than I've ever wanted anything in my life." Tarek blushed and looked away. "God, I sound so needy."

Portland ran his fingers across Tarek's clavicle. He was formed so beautifully. Perfect. It was like he had been born for Portland. "Do you? Because every word you said matches exactly how I feel."

Tarek met his gaze again. Hope lived in his eyes.

Portland skimmed his lips across Tarek's. "Just stay," he whispered between kisses. "Let me show you every day how serious I am."

Tarek kissed him. "Okay." His answer was barely a whisper, but it sounded like a shout to Portland's ears. He hadn't lied. Every word Tarek had said matched the way he felt, and Portland wasn't one to deny himself. Tarek was precious to him. He would be damned if he lost him.

There was still a slight quiver in Tarek's soul. The night had rocked him. The man Tarek had seen in Saul's office scared him a little and turned him on, which was nuts. He hoped Portland didn't turn out to be a crazed abuser. More likely, it took a lion to run an entire banking system. Either way, Saul had said he could come back at any time. Then there was the fact that Portland had dropped fifty grand in his lap like it meant nothing. The guy had been driving around with it in the trunk of his car. That was insane. He couldn't imagine what it must be like to be him. Tarek wanted to crawl under Portland's skin and find out. He couldn't stop using his tongue to toy with Portland's tongue

Damn. He was like some delicious treat Tarek couldn't stop eating.

The doorbell rang.

Portland groaned. "That would be dinner." He looked down at himself and laughed. An erection tented his expensive dress pants. That was the downside of fine materials. They showed too much.

Tarek stood and untucked his shirt. It was long enough to hide any sign of his erection. "I'll grab it."

"Thanks. I tipped the guy in the app, so you should be good."

Tarek winked and made his way to the door. He opened it to find a lanky, red-haired man who looked familiar. There was no food. "Oh. Hi."

A bright smile lit the guy's face. "Hey. Is Portland around?"

"Um." Tarek glanced over his shoulder, more than a little confused. He knew he had seen the guy before. Tarek remembered now. It had been playing cards with Portland. They were obviously close enough friends for the guy to know where he lived.

Before he could decide what to do, Portland stormed the door, looking thunderous. "Excuse me a minute, gorgeous." He stepped around Tarek and headed outside, pulling the door closed behind him.

For a second, Tarek blinked at the wooden surface in confusion before padding back to the couch. He had thought a friend had visited without calling. Now his brain itched with suspicion and jealousy. He fought the urge to press his ear to the door to see what he could hear. It was ridiculous how Portland kept him twisted into knots. Tarek was like a pendulum, swinging from one emotion to the other.

The pair strolled inside.

Portland flashed him a smile. "We'll just be a minute."

Tarek managed his best unbothered expression. "Okay." He watched the pair head down the hall and step inside Portland's home office. He left the door cracked and Tarek lost the battle against his curiosity. As quietly as possible, he made his way down the hall. He already planned to claim he was headed for the bathroom if he got caught, but he didn't want to get caught. Tarek quickly peeked through the crack, hoping they wouldn't spot him. He didn't have to worry. They had their backs to the door. Tarek watched as Portland slid away part of the wall, revealing a floor to ceiling safe. He scanned his fingerprint and retina. Then he punched in a code before the door popped open. Tarek couldn't see what was inside, but it looked like a whole other room. Both men disappeared inside. Tarek returned to the couch, even more confused than before he followed. If Portland owned a safe like that, why drive around with fifty grand in his trunk? Then again, Portland ran an entire east coast banking branch. There was no telling what he had to bring home from work and keep safe. He probably had a lot of responsibility to everything he could access. There wasn't a single reason other than work that would explain things.

The two reappeared.

Their late-night visitor held a leather duffle bag much like the one Portland had given Tarek. He nodded at Tarek and headed for the door without looking back. Had Portland given him money too? What the fuck was happening?

Portland followed the guy out and returned all smiles and carrying their food. "I guess the delivery guy just left it."

Tarek tried for a smile. "That doesn't surprise me. They don't like interacting." He looked past Portland. "Who was that?"

"An employee."

"Oh." Now Tarek felt stupid for being nosey. "I thought he looked familiar. That's the only reason I asked."

Portland carried the bags to the couch. He looked unbothered as he stole a quick kiss. "You're allowed to ask questions." He sat and dug food from the bag. "If we're in this for the long haul, we should be free to talk about anything."

Portland sounded so unconcerned and matter of fact, Tarek's shoulders relaxed. He obviously wasn't worried and wanted this to be real. Tarek let everything go and helped Portland unload the food. They were happy and wanted all the same things. Everything else would fall into place. He just knew it.

CHAPTER SEVEN

TAREK: *I'M NOT COMING home again tonight.*

Salem: *LOL! Why do you keep telling me? At this point, I'll just assume you're not coming home and be pleasantly surprised to see you whenever you do.*

Tarek: *Fair. Love you.*

Salem: *I love you too. The boys say they miss you.*

Tarek: *I miss them too.*

Portland: *I'm in the car. Meetings ran late today. I'll be home as soon as I can.*

Tarek: *It's fine. I ran home and grabbed some more clothes, so I'm just getting back. I can't wait to see you, though.*

Portland: *Same. It was a long day. What else did you do?*

Tarek: *I worked on my book. It's gotten almost long enough to publish. I'm going to be brave and follow your advice to do the indie thing.*

Portland: *Good. You can do anything you set your mind to. I'm proud of you.*

Tarek: *I'm not sure how these cooking lessons are going. You get to be my guinea pig.*

Portland: *I'm sure it'll be great. If not, you've only been at it a month. I believe in you.*

Tarek: *Thanks. I don't. LOL! I just want to make you happy.*

Portland: *By cooking? Baby, I can hire a chef and you can relax all day. That's what I want anyhow.*

Tarek: *Hmm. We'll see if you say the same once you're eating my delicious food.*

Tarek: *That chef you hired won't let me in the kitchen.*

Portland: *Angel, you almost burned down the house.*

Tarek: **pouting**

Portland: *Don't worry. If you're bored, I'll be home soon. I have something I want to talk to you about. Also, I paid for that kitchen. Go in if you want.*

Tarek: *Holy anxiety. Don't you know you're not supposed to tell people you have something to talk to them about later with no context?*

Portland: *I promise it's nothing bad. Did you get to see Salem today?*

Tarek: *Unfortunately, no. He wasn't there when I went home to grab more stuff.*

Portland: *Do you have anything left over there?*

Tarek: *A little. I can take some stuff home, if you'd rather I didn't keep so much here.*

Tarek chewed the side of his thumbnail, waiting for Portland to get home. While Portland claimed what they needed to talk about wasn't bad, he also hadn't responded to Tarek asking if he should take his things home. He kind of wanted to pack his stuff just to be safe. The last thing Tarek wanted was to be forced to gather his belongings while Portland watched. He had known four months together wasn't enough for them to be living together yet. Technically, he didn't live here. Tarek just spent every night and needed his things. It was easier to keep them here. His shoulders fell. He shouldn't have brought so much. It would take him forever to gather everything and likely more than one trip to get it all home.

Warm lips touched the back of his neck.

Tarek's eyes closed as he savored Portland's touch.

"Why are you sitting in the kitchen chewing your nails?"

He released a slow breath as chill bumps formed on his skin. Tarek loved having his neck kissed. "You didn't answer my last text." His voice came out sounding breathless. Tarek never got enough of Portland's touch.

Portland licked a path to Tarek's ear and sucked his earlobe before lightly kissing the shell of his ear. His breath brushed across Tarek's ear while his hand slid down Tarek's stomach. "You're too beautiful to be worrying."

Tarek gripped the edge of the bar where he sat, watching the chef Portland hired to cook for them four nights a week bustle around the kitchen. The poor guy visibly tried to keep his eyes averted and head down.

"We're not alone."

A sexy chuckle rumbled against his ear. "I take it you don't like to be watched?"

Tarek swallowed. He was so turned on. "Not like this."

Portland pulled away. "I didn't answer your text because that's what I wanted to talk to you about. Some things should be done in person."

Tarek's stomach dropped. "I'll take some stuff home." He heard the hurt in his voice and hated himself for it.

Portland spun the stool, forcing Tarek to face him. He moved to stand between Tarek's thighs. "That's not what I want. In fact, I'd prefer the opposite. Let's pick up the rest of your things and make it permanent. This is your home. I'd love for you to admit it."

Tarek was shocked to his core. In a good way. "Really?" There was no missing the hope in his question.

Portland shuffled even closer and hauled Tarek against him. "I love you. This is where you belong. I don't want to worry about the possibility of you sleeping somewhere else again. Your home is with me."

Tarek wanted to cry and shout at the same time. Happiness choked the air from his lungs. It was the first time Portland had said he loved him. Tarek had started worrying he never would, and Tarek couldn't be the first to say it. There was too much of a power imbalance already. He sniffed, holding back happy tears. "I love you too. When I grabbed my things today, I purposely only left one t-shirt so I could say I still have stuff there. It's one I don't even wear."

Portland visibly held back laughter. He looked every bit as happy as Tarek felt. "I have a confession too." He massaged Tarek's thighs. "I maybe did something that'll possibly make you angry."

The immediate sickness in Tarek's gut would have brought him to his knees if he had been standing. "What did you do?" Tarek had no clue how he managed to speak without his voice shaking. A million horrible scenarios ran through his head. If Portland touched someone else, Tarek would die. No exaggeration. That would push him over the edge.

Portland opened his mouth and closed it again. He took Tarek's hand. "Maybe I should just show you."

Tarek had to step over a leather duffle bag next to the stool to follow Portland.

Portland led him to the garage. The lights flared to life as the door opened.

Tarek took a cursory glance before he planned to ask Portland what in the hell was going on, but something was missing. It took him a second to realize why he had experienced such an immediate feeling of loss. His car was gone.

"Where in the hell is my car?"

"Sorry, angel. That thing was on its last leg. I sold it and put the money in your account."

All Tarek could do was stare at Portland in disbelief. He had too many questions and angry words to say. It was like too many people trying to fit through a door. Not a single word would break loose.

Portland chuckled and kissed him. "If you could see your face. It's obvious you intend to kill me, but maybe wait." He took Tarek's hand and led him to where his car should be. A bright blue Audi R56 Avant sat parked in his bay. "I got you something else."

Tarek blinked. The car was fucking beautiful, but he still didn't know how to feel. Portland always dropped things on him. This wasn't like a bag full of cash. Tarek could leave that behind if he needed to leave. This car truly belonged to Portland. He wasn't oblivious. Portland was slowly making him more and more dependent on him. Truthfully, since he lived there now, the car represented the final piece of his life before Portland.

With the one thing he truly owned gone, everything belonged to Portland now, including Tarek.

"I worried about this."

Tarek tore his gaze away from the car and focused on Portland. He looked hurt.

Portland shoved his hands in his pockets. "I swear, I only want to keep you safe. It's fully in your name alone. You don't have to worry that I'm trying to steal your independence or anything. It's completely yours—free and clear."

He was so adorably worried. There wasn't a chance Tarek could be upset with him. Despite his initial fear, he knew Portland had a gorgeous heart and always had the best of intentions. He was a good man. Tarek wrapped his arms around his waist and squeezed, hugging him as tightly as possible.

"Thank you. I know your heart was in the right place, and I'm not worried. Nothing is ever going to come between us, so it doesn't matter anyhow." Parts of that were true. There was enough truth in Tarek's words to let the rest go. It wasn't worth fighting over and it was a gorgeous car. He didn't have any sort of attachment to the old one. It had always gotten him from point A to point B. Otherwise, it was just a car. Portland's feelings mattered more.

Portland hugged him back. He kissed the top of Tarek's head. "Do you want to take her for a spin?"

Tarek shook his head. "Not right now. Right now, I want to make love to the sweetest man alive."

Tarek listened as Portland's chuckle rumbled against his ear. "Tell me his name. I'll have him killed."

A smile exploded across Tarek's face. "Is it crazy that I'm happier about you saying you love me than I am about the car?"

Portland pushed him against the SUV parked next to his new car. It happened so quickly, Tarek lost his breath. Portland's eyes flashed with something deadly. The dark Portland was back. A thrill of excitement ran down Tarek's spine as Portland's mouth covered his. A moan immediately rose in his throat. Portland swallowed it. Their kiss turned more heated by the second. Tarek tore at the buttons on Portland's expensive dress shirt.

Portland pulled away and yanked open the back door of the SUV. Tarek didn't hesitate to climb inside. Portland followed, lowering the bench back seat into a functional bed as he went. He closed them inside. Tarek was beneath him in a matter of seconds. God, he was amazing. The way he used his tongue always rocked Tarek. He had talent and years of practice. Portland never failed to use those against him.

They tore at each other until their bare chests met, and then everything slowed. Their kiss turned loving. Tarek didn't rush as he set Portland's erection free. The moment Tarek's fingertips skimmed Portland's cock, Portland sat back on his heels and dug out his wallet. Tarek didn't hesitate to scramble out the rest of his clothes. His patience was gone. Portland found the small packet of lube and condom Tarek had made him start carrying. They had missed an opportunity outside Portland's office one day thanks to Portland not having anything with him, and Tarek had forgotten his wallet. Portland lubed Tarek first. He teased Tarek as he did, stretching and massaging all the right places. Tarek snapped. He went on the attack. He pushed Portland on to his back and straddled him. Tarek wasn't thinking. He wanted Portland too badly. In an instant, he sat on Portland's dick.

Portland made a sound like a dying man.

Tarek froze as he realized what he had done.

There was no condom between them.

They held each other's stare. Then Portland slowly lured Tarek down into a kiss. His gaze never wavered until their lips met. Tarek rocked, testing the waters. Their tongues brushed. A silent agreement was made. It didn't matter. They were forever. This was permanent. Nothing could break them.

Just like their rush to make love, the tension built quickly. The sounds Portland made were too hot. He made Tarek feel sexy as hell and aroused him beyond what he could bear. Tarek worked harder to reach the edge.

"Shit, Tarek. You're killing me. I love you so much." He sucked Tarek's neck. "Jesus. I was so scared you would leave me over the car. It would kill me if I lost you."

Even as Tarek wound tighter, his eyes filled with tears. He hadn't known he could love a person so much. "I could never leave you. It'd be like ripping out my own heart." Tarek sucked in a breath and held it. His muscles tensed. The pressure became too much. Ecstasy washed over him. A cry tore from his throat. "I love you. Goddamn, Portland. I love you so much." He honestly didn't even know what he said anymore. Tarek was in heaven. His body shook. Cum coated Portland's sexy torso. Portland cried out beneath him. The sound of their pleasure echoed inside the car. Steam covered the windows. Portland pulled him in for another kiss. It tasted desperate, as if they still hadn't managed to get close enough to each other. Tarek no longer knew what their intentions had been toward each other when they met. But he knew it no longer mattered, because what they had found overshadowed every plan. This was real love. It was everything.

Portland carried a very content Tarek inside and put him to bed. Wearing only his pants, he headed for the kitchen and found the chef packing up to leave. The guy barely glanced his way. His gaze landed briefly on Portland's newly acquired hickey before he looked away again. Portland got the feeling he wouldn't be keeping the guy. While he came highly recommended and his meals were passable, Portland got the impression he was either homophobic or simply didn't like Portland. Either way, Portland would be damned if he felt uncomfortable in his own home.

Portland grabbed their dinner plates, nodded at the guy, and headed back down the hall. He had already gently cleaned his baby. Now, he would feed him. Life with Tarek was more than he dreamed. Looking back, he couldn't believe he thought he would simply buy Tarek. Tarek truly didn't care about his money. He always accepted Portland's decisions and gifts, but it was beyond obvious he only did so to make Portland happy. He didn't give two shits about a new car. This was real love. It was almost laughable the way he had gone from thinking love didn't exist to being swept away by innocence. But here they were, and Portland couldn't be more content.

He had never had sex without a condom. Until it happened with Tarek, Portland hadn't realized it had been more about waiting to be totally settled than it was about protecting himself. The moment Tarek had sat on his cock with nothing between them, Portland saw his entire future unfold. Tarek was there for every second of it. This was it for him. They were the last relationship he would ever have. Tarek was his final partner. This was forever.

He found Tarek right where he left him. Tarek sat up at the sight of food. "Mmm. I'm starving. Ezra said the pasta would melt in our mouths."

"Who's Ezra?"

Tarek laughed at his confusion. "The chef."

"Oh." Portland climbed onto the bed with their plates. "I'm probably going to fire the guy."

Tarek nodded, looking unsurprised. "He doesn't seem to care for you for whatever reason. It's uncomfortable."

Portland was more than a little relieved to hear Tarek wouldn't fight him on the matter. He handed Tarek a plate.

Tarek took a bite of whatever the dish was. He immediately set the plate on the bedside table. "Would you like to order pizza?"

A laugh burst from Portland. "Dislike aside, the guy is supposed to be a five-star chef." He took a bite. A bitter flavor filled his mouth. He spit it back out. "Yeah. That's nasty. What the hell? Maybe we don't have five-star taste." They looked at each other and burst into laughter. It hit Portland. He was more than in love with Tarek. Tarek was his best friend.

Marry me. The thought was so loud, it nearly left Portland's lips. He stopped at the last second. Tarek deserved more than an impromptu marriage proposal in bed. "I have a meeting in the morning, but we should spend the day together afterward. We could have a street fair day, eat truck food, and ride the carousel."

Tarek's smile never dimmed. "That sounds amazing. I can't picture you eating truck food, though."

Portland laughed. "I don't know why. We're about to order the world's greasiest pizza."

Tarek's gaze moved over Portland's face. He leaned his head back against the headboard—like settling in to simply stare at Portland. "I love you." He sounded so serious, a lump immediately formed in Portland's throat.

"I love you too." Portland moved to his knees and made a show of crawling Tarek's way.

A worried look settled on Tarek's face. "Oh no."

Portland nodded. "You look like a man who needs a tickle."

Tarek pulled up his knees. "No." Laughter tinted his voice.

Portland snagged his legs and yanked, pulling him down the bed. He pretended to tickle his ribs while straddling Tarek's body. Portland didn't put any real effort into it. He hated being tickled and meant the moment to be playful. Tarek squirmed beneath him, playing along. Portland used the opportunity to steal the kiss he wanted. While their tongues played, Portland plotted. He would borrow one of Tarek's rings he had left on the bathroom counter, so he could get a size. Tarek would get a proper proposal. They would have a happy life. Portland would make damn sure of that. First, he had a terrible chef to fire.

CHAPTER EIGHT

THE COMPETING SMELLS OF fried foods mixed in the air, leaving an indecipherable odor of grease. It reminded Portland of his teenage years. They were a long time ago, but the fair was one of his good memories. He held Tarek's hand while Tarek tried looking at everything at once.

"Have you never been here?"

At Portland's question, Tarek looked his way. "No. I've only lived here a couple of years. Honestly, I still don't feel confident driving without my GPS, much less have I done a ton of exploring. This is great, though." He laughed. "I still don't see this being a place you'd hang out."

"I grew up in this town," Portland reminded him. "While my parents definitely weren't the type to take their son to the fair, my friends loved to hang out here. We would spend whole weekends at the fair, trying to pick up chicks."

A loud bark of laughter burst from Tarek. He covered his mouth to stifle the sound, but his eyes sparkled with humor. After a second, he pulled his hand away just enough to speak. "You picked up chicks?"

Portland chuckled at Tarek's reaction. "Of course. You have to remember, being gay wasn't openly accepted back then

Like any teenager, I wanted to fit in with my friends." He winked. "One of them knew the truth, though."

Tarek shook his head. "I have the hardest time picturing you as a teenager. You never really talk much about yourself, much less your childhood."

"To be fair, you don't talk about your childhood either. I understand, though. I'm sure it's hard to talk about your parents."

Tarek looked away for a second, making Portland wish he hadn't said anything. When Tarek looked back, he seemed okay. "Are your parents still alive?"

Portland shook his head. "They both died pretty young, actually. My mom died when I was a senior in high school. She had some rare and silent form of cancer.

They didn't even know about it until the autopsy. At least she didn't suffer. My dad remarried less than a year later. Thankfully, he had an ironclad prenup. When he died less than a decade later, she tried to fight me for everything my mother had built."

Tarek's eyebrows rose. "Your mother was the wealthy one?"

Portland nodded. "She came from old money. They hated my dad and cut her off until I was born. Since she was used to being wealthy, she did everything she could to build her own empire. Once I was born and my grandparents had a grandchild to consider, she was cut back into the family's money as well. They didn't want me going without. So, really, the money Dad's wife tried to get was mine. I was just trying to be nice after I turned twenty-one by letting my dad stay in the home he had lived in since he married my mom. But technically, everything he owned was mine. Mom left everything to me. My grandparents would've never let it be any other way, even if Mom hadn't managed to build her own fortune."

"Are either of your grandparents still alive?"

Portland smiled. "My grandmother is. I'm pretty sure she intends to outlive us all. She's ninety-three and still lives at home, running the place like a queen." He looked Tarek's way. "She'll love you."

Tarek's eyebrows rose. "Do you really believe that, or are you humoring me? Surely, if she hated your dad, she'll take one look at me and assume I'm a gold digger."

He squeezed Tarek's hand. "Nah. Everyone hated my dad because he was a serial cheater. My grandma is one of those sickeningly sweet people. Under normal circumstances, she loves everyone, but you're especially her type."

"How so?" Tarek sounded genuinely curious.

"You're a born giver. All it takes is one look at you to see you're the type of person who will give someone the shirt off their back if you care about them."

Tarek looked away. "I hope that's true." He looked back. His eyes sparkled. "I'd give you any clothes you wanted."

Portland shook his head at his antics. He loved Tarek so goddamn much. No one else set him free to relax and let his guard down. No one else in his life was good. Portland spotted the Ferris wheel.

He pulled Tarek toward it. "Come on. We have to ride this one."

Tarek shrugged. "Sounds good to me."

The second Tarek turned his back, Portland handed the man operating the ride fifty bucks. The guy knew what it was for without Portland asking. They strapped in and the wheel slowly spun, lifting them into the air. The moment they reached the highest point, the wheel stopped.

Tarek glanced around. "Wow. It's beautiful up here."

Portland's gaze never wavered from Tarek even as he dug the ring he had bought that morning from his pocket. "It is."

Tarek turned his head and met his gaze. They stared at each other, and Portland knew this was right.

"I did something as cliche as possible."

A smile exploded across Tarek's lips. "What's that? I can't see you doing anything like anyone else."

Portland was suddenly too nervous to laugh. He wanted this too badly to let that stop him. "I gave the guy fifty bucks to stop the ride when we got to the top."

"Nice. How long do we get to stay up here?"

Portland held up the velvet box he hid. "Long enough for this. Will you marry me?"

Tarek's eyes immediately filled with tears. He covered his mouth and blinked several times. A minute passed before Tarek dropped his hands and sniffed. "Are you serious? You're really asking me to marry you right now? Is this a fever dream?"

A nervous laugh escaped Portland. He didn't know if this was a good reaction or a bad one. "I'm really asking." He realized he hadn't opened the box.

Before he could, Tarek grabbed the collar of his shirt and yanked him across the seat. His mouth covered Portland's with a desperation Portland had never seen from Tarek. By the time he pulled away, Portland realized he should have paid the guy a hundred to make sure they didn't come down until Portland could get off this ride without embarrassing himself.

"Yes."

Portland blinked. Tarek had fucked with his mind so hard with that kiss, it took him a second to realize Tarek accepted. "Seriously?" Even he heard the disbelief in his voice. Until Tarek said yes, he hadn't realized how crazy anyone would be to marry him... especially a particularly sweet man who knew nothing about the real him.

As Tarek laughed and opened the ring box, Portland made a vow. Tarek would never know. Whatever it took, he would never let Tarek see the dark side of his life. Everything would always be beautiful for him. This one thing would stay pure.

Tarek practically levitated with happiness. He wanted to dance. Tarek wanted to tell everyone they passed. He wanted to start planning a wedding. Of course, he didn't even know if Portland wanted a wedding. His mind bounced all over the place as they drove home. He was afraid to open his mouth and have a squeal pop out.

Tarek counted to ten and took a breath. "So, did you have a plan?"

Portland cast a quick glance his way. "What do you mean?"

A nervous chuckle escaped. "Um. Like, do you want a long engagement or a short one? Did you want a big wedding or to elope? Am I moving you too fast?"

Portland chuckled. It was one of his sexy deep ones that made butterflies stir in Tarek's stomach. "I asked you. You're not moving me too fast. I'm happy to let you decide on the wedding details, though. If you want a big one, that's what we'll do. If you just want to elope or do a small destination wedding with just us, that's what we'll do. I just want to marry you. My only request is that we have a short engagement. I can't tell you how many times I've rolled my eyes when people tell me they're engaged, and it's been like eight years. Boy, you're not engaged. They're pacifying you while they wait for someone better."

Even though Portland spoke with a hint of humor, that opinion sounded personal. He wondered if Portland felt strung along by someone at some point. Thankfully, Tarek had found his perfect match. He didn't want to wait. "Honestly? Please don't think I'm crazy. I'd love to have as short of an engagement as possible without missing out on some sort of wedding. The destination thing sounds nice. Of course, I'm sure you'll want some sort of prenup and I don't know how long those take."

Portland shot him an annoyed look. "I don't want a prenup. I've made it this long without getting married for a reason. This is something I'm only doing once, and it's 'til death do we part, one way or the other."

Tarek laughed. "Okay. Sounds fair. I'd be okay with one, though. It's always been important to me that you know

I'm not in this for the money, but yeah. Prenups always have made me wonder why they bothered getting married when they started out expecting divorce. But I won't be offended if you feel like you need to protect yourself."

Portland took his hand and brought it to his lips. He placed a light kiss on Tarek's knuckles. "I've never been surer of anything or anyone in my life. You're the one for me."

Tarek's heart soared.

"Plus, when your books take off, you'll probably wish you'd protected yourself from me."

He was so sweet. They both knew Tarek's books wouldn't go anywhere. "Never. This is forever, one way or the other."

Portland shot him a laughing look.

They pulled into the garage and climbed from the car. Tarek swore he felt the heat build between them as they headed inside. He knew he was right when neither of them attempted to stop anywhere else as they made their way to the bedroom. Tarek emptied his pockets onto the bedside table. He caught sight of the engagement ring on his finger and smiled. It fit perfectly. Tarek wasn't sure how Portland pulled that off, but he wasn't surprised. Portland was always calculated in every step he made. He never moved without purpose. The ring was fucking gorgeous. He didn't doubt for a second it cost at least five figures. The man spent too much money on him.

Portland's hands found his hips. He dragged Tarek back against his chest. His lips explored Tarek's neck. "Do you like it?"

"I love it."

"I love you." He tugged Tarek's shirt upward and stole it. After tossing it aside, his hands slid up Tarek's torso while his mouth enjoyed Tarek's ear. "Oh." Portland took a step back. "Strip. I have another surprise for you. Maybe it's a bit of a gift for me," he said with a wicked-sounding chuckle.

"You spoil me too much." Despite his halfhearted argument, Tarek scrambled from his clothes. He sat on the bed.

Portland made a gesture for him to turn around. "There's no such thing as spoiling you too much."

Tarek moved to the center of the bed and turned his back on Portland. He heard a lot of shuffling around, including Portland's belt being removed and his zipper being unzipped. Tarek nearly shivered with anticipation. He had no clue what Portland's surprise could be.

The bed dipped behind him. "While I waited for the jeweler to make some adjustments, I saw something else." A pearl necklace appeared in front of him as Portland reached around to put the necklace on him.

Tarek gasped. It was beautiful and definitely real. There were a lot of pearls, and he was blown away. The piece draped over his clavicle and poured down his chest.

Portland kissed his shoulder as he ran his fingers over the piece. "I knew I had to see this against your skin. You have no idea how much your neck fascinates me." His lips swept down Tarek's nape. "It should be draped in something beautiful."

Tarek thought he might cry. "You do way too much for me, and I don't even know how to return the favor. I want to spoil you too. I want to make you feel special the way you do for me."

"You have no idea how special you make me feel." Portland shifted positions and eased Tarek onto his back. He straddled Tarek. "There's no way you can know what it's like to have you love me for real. It's not an act, and it's so fucking beautiful. Every day, I wake up and you're still here and I'm floored. You can have anyone and yet you choose me. I know there have been plenty of times you should've run from me, but you didn't. You just love me, purely and completely. There's no way you can know," he repeated.

A tear slipped from the corner of Tarek's eye and slid back into his hair. His breath stuttered when he tried to speak. "I love you more than anything. In my eyes, you're perfect."

"And that's priceless to me," Portland whispered as he brushed his lips across Tarek's. As his full weight lowered onto him, Tarek knew Portland settled in for the long haul and this would be a long night. That sounded like heaven to him.

CHAPTER NINE

TAREK TRAILED FROM ROOM to room, walking on clouds. Portland had a meeting, but he had kept it to only one again today. It would likely take half the day, but they would still get extra time together. Portland's leather duffle still sat on the kitchen floor where Tarek had stepped over it the other night. He grabbed it and hauled it to the bedroom before someone tripped and killed themselves. That someone being him. As he dropped the bag on the bench at the end of the bed, the doorbell rang. As far as Tarek knew, there wasn't anyone scheduled to come by today. It wasn't a normal cleaning day and the landscape people had just been there two days ago. He made his way to the front door. As always, Tarek checked the peephole. A police officer stood on the other side. Fear shot through Tarek. Had Portland been in an accident? He practically tore open the door. The middle-aged brown-haired cop looked a little surprised at the sight of Tarek, which he found odd.

"Can I help you?"

"Is Portland Wales here?"

Tarek shook his head. "He's working today."

The guy held up a piece of paper. "We have a warrant to search the premises."

Everything inside Tarek went on full alert and in guard dog mode. This was his home to protect when Portland wasn't there. Plus, he had a bit of anger issues with police being used against him. That had been one of his parents' favorite tactics: claiming Salem held him against his will.

"Let me see it, then."

Tarek continued blocking the path while he read the warrant. "This warrant is only for the kitchen." He lifted his chin and locked eyes with the cop. "You can bet damn well I'll be watching every step to ensure that's where you'll stay." He pointed toward the side of the house. "Round that corner and meet me at that door. It leads to the kitchen. You won't be stepping inside any other room."

The guy looked a little proud of Tarek for some reason. "Yes, sir." It was a sarcastic agreement, but Tarek didn't care. They weren't friends.

Tarek closed the door and internally panicked. He needed to call Portland. Why in the hell was there a warrant to search any part of their house? He dialed Portland's number as he moved to the kitchen door.

Portland answered on the second ring. "Hello?"

"The police are here with a search warrant. It's real. I checked it, but it's only for the kitchen. I'm letting them in through the side door, so they won't have an excuse to check anywhere else." He spoke quickly. The words poured from him in his panic.

Thankfully, Portland stayed calm. "I'm over an hour away, but I'm turning around. Do not answer a single question." Portland emphasized every word. "I'll call my attorney. Shaw can get there faster than I can. Anything they ask, tell them your lawyer is on the way and will handle anything they need to know. Don't worry, baby. I'll take care of this."

Tarek squared his shoulders. He was a lot stronger than he looked. "I got this until the lawyer gets here."

"Good boy. I love you. Just hang tight."

Tarek disconnected the call and let the police in. A lot more cops than he expected poured in. Tarek immediately moved to the kitchen doorway, blocking the way to the sitting room, where he could ensure no one moved outside the warrant zone.

The man who issued the warrant stayed glued to Tarek. "So you are..."

Tarek held his stare, ensuring the guy knew he was serious. "Waiting for my lawyer."

"Your lawyer? So I assume you're the son or..."

Tarek rolled his eyes.

"Yeah. I get it, but I'm just asking for a name. I'm Bryan."

Tarek still refused to respond.

"What do you think I can do with your name?"

With a sigh, Tarek partially lost the battle. "I have no idea, but you're in my house for no reason, so you tell me. What can you do with a name?"

A tall guy in a very expensive suit stepped through the door the police had left open. He scanned the room and then headed straight for Tarek.

"You've got to be fucking shitting me," Bryan muttered under his breath.

Tarek smirked. He knew Portland would have a lawyer that left people quaking in their boots.

The sound of silverware hitting the floor assaulted Tarek's ears. Tarek cringed.

Shaw's gaze shot toward the ruckus. "You'd better take care because you will be picking up whatever mess you make. I can guarantee that."

Tarek's smile grew at Shaw's firmly spoken promise.

He focused on Bryan. "Kindly move away so I can speak with my client."

With a muscle jumping in his jaw, Bryan moved out of earshot.

Shaw focused surprisingly sweet-looking dark green eyes on him. "Did you say anything?"

Tarek shook his head. "I just checked the warrant and saw it was for only the kitchen. So I made them come in through the side door so they couldn't claim they spotted something in another room. Then I moved to right here to ensure they didn't step foot past the warrant's zone."

One corner of Shaw's mouth lifted. Tarek had to tilt his chin up to hold the guy's stare. He looked smart and capable. Tarek was grateful as hell he was there. Shaw squeezed his shoulder. "Just stay here a minute and let me find out what's going on."

Tarek nodded.

Shaw found Bryan. They spoke in low tones for a minute before he returned to Tarek's side. Tarek took great pleasure in seeing the cops picking up their mess as they went. Shaw hovered over him again. "Do you have any thoughts on who could or would claim they found more than a kilo of cocaine packaged for distribution in a duffle bag in the kitchen?"

Tarek blinked. "What the fuck?" He shook his head. "No one has been here."

His mind reeled and then sped. Holy shit. The duffle bag. There was no fucking way. Who else had even seen it, much less in their kitchen? It hit him. "Wait. I take that back. Our chef. Portland fired him yesterday. Maybe this was his way of getting back at us."

Shaw nodded. "That sounds good to me. It's something I can use." He glanced around. "Why don't you hang out in another room out of sight? I've got this. You have nothing to worry about. I'll make sure these guys leave and ensure they pick up any mess they make. Nothing will come of this."

Tarek nodded. There was a huge lump in his throat. "Thank you, and it's nice to meet you."

A sexy smile exploded across Shaw's face. "It's nice to meet you too and congratulations on your upcoming nuptials."

Tarek nodded again and awkwardly walked away. He was more than a little surprised people already knew about the engagement, and he hoped those nuptials were still a thing. The sick feeling in the pit of his stomach said otherwise. He stepped inside the bedroom he shared with someone he feared he didn't know. His gaze landed on the duffle bag. He closed the door. For much longer than necessary, he stared at the bag before gathering the courage to move closer. He took a shaky breath and grabbed the zipper. He already knew in his heart his entire world would shatter with a single glance. There was no going back from here.

A million thoughts ran through Portland's mind. He had gotten too comfortable in his own home. That duffle bag was still in the kitchen. He needed to get ahead of that. Why had he been searched in the first place? He was supposed to be protected. That was the first fucking call he made the moment he got off the phone with Shaw. Prince Noir would damn well fix this, or Portland would bring the whole kingdom down. He knew he had made his bed, but Tarek slept in that bed too now. No one would tarnish his angel.

By the time he made it home, the police were gone and only Shaw remained. "Where's Tarek?"

Shaw motioned toward the hallway. "I believe he's holed up in the bedroom."

At least he was here. "What did they find?"

"Nothing."

Portland swiped his hand over his eyes. "I'm sorry about all this. Obviously, I've gotten complacent."

Shaw made a dismissive gesture. "You never had anything to worry about. The local police are nothing and this Bryan guy who managed a warrant has zero authority. There isn't a single person of importance we don't own. This was only a minor inconvenience."

It was easy for Shaw to say that. The blown apart pieces of his relationship weren't waiting in the bedroom. He shifted from foot to foot. His gaze slid toward the hall.

"He was brave as hell. You should've seen him. They didn't know how to handle him. He guarded this house like a champ."

Portland swallowed. "He doesn't know."

Shaw winced. He slapped Portland's shoulder and squeezed. "Well, I'll let you deal with that one. That's above my skill set."

Portland nodded and managed a smile. "Thank you for showing up and keeping him safe until I got here."

Shaw smiled like they were old friends. "It's no problem. Despite whatever you're facing now, I envy you. He was the one in charge when I arrived. You've got a strong one. He can handle this."

That was the problem. Portland never wanted him to. He flashed a pained smile. "We'll see soon enough, I'm sure. I might need you again in few minutes. If he kills me, I'd still like you to defend him."

Shaw shook his head and headed for the door. With a final goodbye, Portland locked up and made his way down the hall. The bedroom door was closed. He wondered if it would be locked against him. The handle easily turned beneath his hand. As he stepped through the door, Tarek looked up from his spot in the center of the bed. The covers were piled around him, as if he was cold. The

TV played his favorite cartoon with no sound. His eyes and nose were red. It was beyond obvious he had been crying. Portland's heart shattered. He never wanted to be the reason Tarek cried.

Tarek turned back the covers, revealing the leather duffle bag. "I had just brought it to the bedroom to get it out of the middle of the floor when the doorbell rang."

Fuck. His voice sounded so small. Portland moved closer and sat on the edge of the bed. "Did you open it?"

Tarek squeezed the leather, as if needing something to give him strength. "I almost did, but I couldn't bring myself to do it. There's a terrible feeling in my gut, telling me this bag could destroy us, and I'm not strong enough." He passed the bag to Portland. "I don't want to know."

Portland took the bag from him and set it on his lap. He stared down at the leather. It was specially designed to block the smell of drugs. Nearly a hundred thousand dollars' worth of cocaine was inside and Portland was so desensitized, he had forgotten it for two days in the kitchen. He didn't want to ruin them, but he also didn't want secrets to destroy them. "It's okay if you want to look inside."

A sweet smile touched Tarek's lips. "I know, and that's exactly why I don't want to." He drew his knees up and wrapped his arms around them. "It probably makes me look weak or stupid, but you're all I have. I mean, I know I can always count on Salem, but it's not the same. For as long as I lived with Salem, and as much as I adore him, I never felt at home. Honestly, I don't think I've felt at home my entire life. Then I met you. You're my home. If seeing what's inside that bag costs me you, then I can't do it. The price is too high."

Portland couldn't believe he argued, but this was genuine love. "What if the not knowing ends up killing your love for me? What happens if you spend the rest of your life questioning my every move and wondering what I'm hiding? Losing you would kill me no matter how it happens, but I can't watch your love for me slowly die."

Tarek slipped from the bed and took the bag from Portland. He held it in one hand and took Portland's hand with the other. Portland stood and let Tarek lead him down the hall. He made his way inside Portland's office. Portland watched as Tarek set the bag aside and pushed aside the false wall, revealing the room-sized safe behind it. He realized Tarek had never been as oblivious as he thought.

Tarek motioned toward the locked safe. "Show me how to unlock it."

Portland had no idea where this was headed, but he didn't hesitate to do as told. He set the safe to add a user. "Come here." Portland led him through the retina scan and fingerprint. They set a code for Tarek together. Then the door swung open.

Tarek didn't go inside. He turned his back on the room and held out the bag. "You should put this away. I have access now. This isn't a secret. You're not hiding anything from me. I'm just not getting involved."

Damn. He was amazing. Portland moved to take the bag.

Tarek pulled it back and hesitated. "Tell me one thing, though. Are you in any danger? When you walk out that door every day, do I need to be scared?"

Portland closed the distance between them and wrapped his arms around Tarek. "I swear to you that I'm perfectly safe. Under no circumstances would I endanger you or us. I want us too badly. Nothing matters to me as much as this relationship. You're not the only one who felt empty and alone when we met." He kissed Tarek's temple. "You're all I have too."

Tarek squeezed him. He felt Tarek nod. "Okay. I want to make sure everything got put back where it goes in the kitchen.

If not, I want Shaw to destroy someone. Right after he presses charges against the stupid chef."

The chef part was new information, but it made sense. They had left him alone with the bag the night before Portland fired him. The words of a disgruntled employee didn't carry a lot of weight, thankfully. "I'll make sure it's taken care of. Check on the kitchen. I'll be there in a minute."

Tarek kissed his throat and stepped around him, leaving Portland alone. Portland stuffed the bag on the shelf with several identical ones. He turned in a circle and eyed the room. A cache of weapons covered one wall. He was glad Tarek wanted access. Now Portland knew he would have the means to defend himself if need be. He reset the safe and slid the wall back into place. The weight on his chest still hadn't eased. He had never been more scared of losing someone. There was a real possibility he still could.

Portland rounded the corner into the kitchen and found Tarek bustling from cabinet to cabinet. He paused and leaned against the door frame to watch. Tarek was so incredibly beautiful inside and out. He didn't belong with someone like Portland. But Portland was one of the bad guys, so he had no intention of letting him go.

"What about Zakynthos? There are these caves there over the most beautiful water you've ever seen. They also have a gorgeous wedding venue."

Tarek turned, looking thoughtful. "I was thinking about a beach wedding. I don't know where that is, though."

"Greece."

Tarek brightened. "I love that. As you know, my mom is from there. Even though she's crazy, and I have very mixed feelings about my family, I've always wanted to visit."

There was a lump the size of a softball in Portland's throat. He was afraid to hope Tarek's forgiveness was real. "It's gorgeous this time of year."

The hope that lit Tarek's features nearly broke Portland. "You want to go now?"

Portland nodded. He was beyond speech, but he tried. His voice broke when he spoke. "I can't let you get away."

Tarek crossed the room and wrapped his arms around Portland. He buried his face against his throat. Every breath he took brushed his skin. "Okay." His cold nose pressed even closer. Portland felt him inhale. "I love that smell. Every time I catch a hint of your scent, I feel so safe and loved. Happy. Let's do it."

A tear slid down Portland's cheek before he could stop it. He swiped it away and sniffed. His hold tightened on Tarek. "You'll always be first and cherished and adored."

"I know."

Portland closed his eyes and took in Tarek's scent. He got what Tarek meant about smelling his skin. Portland lived for the heat of Tarek's neck and the way his skin felt against his lips. He always breathed in Tarek's cologne and felt everything. Every emotion he had searched for years to find overcame him.

No matter what it took, Tarek would be the happiest man alive. Forever. No compromise.

CHAPTER TEN

SALEM WATCHED TAREK AND Portland interact with all the skepticism his bitter heart could muster. He knew Portland's every little dirty secret. Salem had known since before he chose the guy for Tarek. Tarek was the sweetest and most forgiving person alive. Portland was his perfect balance. As the highest-ranking member of Prince Noir's drug empire, Portland had money, power, and connections that matched Salem's. Salem had billions, and that trumped any sort of illegal bullshit. But Salem never scoffed at the crime game either. Someone had to make that money, and Salem adored money. It was truly a boy's best friend. Plus, Portland would take care of Tarek. Salem didn't give a shit how.

Despite having set Tarek in Portland's path, Salem still felt the need to watch them in action. Study them. Measure Portland's strength and worth. Tarek was one of the very few people he loved. The guy was just too damn much to ignore. He loved too much and saw the good in everyone. Tarek needed protection. Portland was the man for the job. He was cold-blooded and ruthless. When he looked at Tarek, Portland was the opposite of his nature in every way. It was fascinating. He was relieved to have

Tarek married and settled. Salem didn't like thinking about other people. Tarek forced him to look too often at his sentimental side. That was a weakness Salem couldn't stand.

Quest poked his head over Salem's shoulder and followed his line of sight to where Tarek sat on Portland's lap on the lounge chair by the pool. "Are you jealous?"

Salem snorted as he reached up to scratch Quest's head—like a pet. The guy loved it. "Of what?"

"They're in love."

"Mhmm. That's nice for Tarek, but I'm not built like that, babe."

"But you love me," Quest said, sounding like a kicked puppy.

Salem kissed his cheek. "I do. Very much."

Quest's usual happy expression returned. "See? I knew it. You love me," he sang, making Salem laugh. Quest and Dodge were so simple. They were uncomplicated. The pair were straight and didn't want Salem for anything more than whatever it was that kept their pure souls running. They were nothing like him. Thank God.

Dodge pulled himself up and out of the pool and jogged their way at Quest's antics. "Wait. I want love too." He dove onto Salem's lounge chair, soaking him with his giant body.

Salem squealed from the sudden cold burst of water. "Holy shit, Dodge. You're too fucking big to jump on top of people.

By people, I mean me." He tried pushing him away. "I can't breathe."

"Pshh." Dodge placed loud kisses all over Salem's face. "You're doing a lot of bitching for someone who can't breathe."

Salem immediately went limp.

Dodge leaped from the lounge chair. "Oh, shit. Are you hurt?"

Salem burst out laughing.

Dodge's expression shifted from worried to playful when he realized Salem had tricked him. He exchanged a glance with Quest. His eyes lit with wickedness. Too late, Salem realized his mistake. He had poked the wrong bear.

Before he could run, he was over Dodge's shoulder. Dodge ran for the pool with Quest hot on their heels. He knew before he hit the water that he would have to let them have their way and play. When he had kept JD's giant puppies after his death, he had known what he was in for. That was okay. They were the best thing about his life. He would die for them.

Portland watched Salem try to hold his own against the two giant children. He shook his head. If there had ever been three people more oblivious, he had never seen it. He was glad to have them in Greece, nonetheless. They were the closest thing to family Tarek had. It had been nice to have them there, supporting Tarek while they said their vows. They were married. He still couldn't believe it. His arms tightened around Tarek. Tarek snuggled closer and kissed his neck. They would likely have some crazy tan lines later, but it was worth it.

Shaw claimed the lounge chair next to them. His gaze locked on the pool. "They're a nice-looking throuple."

Tarek laughed.

Portland explained. "They're a caustic brat and two guys who think they're straight."

Shaw snorted.

They exchanged knowing grins.

Tarek hummed. "Do you really think they're more? That's a nice thought. Salem doesn't let people in."

"Salem? As in Salem Rochester?"

"The one and only," Portland answered, so Tarek wouldn't have to. He knew Tarek got sick of that reaction.

Shaw didn't respond right away. When he did, he sounded pragmatic rather than judgmental. "I can see it. JD did always love a pretty face. It was his greatest dream to scandalize the community by leaving his billions to a young handful." He looked Tarek's way. "No offense to your friend."

Tarek laughed. "None taken. That's an apt description."

Shaw watched the three for a moment longer. He stood. "Well, if the pups want to be straight. I should throw my hat in the ring." He winked before heading toward the ruckus. Shaw dove into the pool, leaving them alone again.

Beneath the cover of the towel Portland had draped over them, protecting them from the slight chill in the breeze, Tarek scraped his fingers down Portland's torso. "So sexy."

Portland immediately went hard. "You're playing with fire, little one."

An evil chuckle vibrated from the bundle against his chest. "Who teased me with Ezra as an audience?"

"Who?"

Tarek huffed.

"I'm just fucking with you. That's the gardener, right?"

He laughed harder when Tarek growled. Tarek got the last laugh. He blatantly cupped Portland's dick through his shorts and squeezed just enough to make Portland bite back a moan.

"Evil."

Tarek lifted his head and met Portland's stare. "Why? I'm completely serious about making you feel good."

He didn't need to hear anything else. It took nothing to scoop Tarek into his arms and dip into their honeymoon hut. The place they had bought out for the next two weeks was a private area with several luxury huts surrounding a pool that looked like paradise, with its waterfalls and greenery. Each guest had their privacy, but they were close enough to also enjoy their company. Tarek and he were the only ones staying after the first week. So they would have complete solitude soon, but not until after they shared their joy with their friends. It was the perfect substitute for an overpriced wedding that lasted a few hours. This was memories for a lifetime, especially the memories he made with Tarek beneath him.

It took nothing to have Tarek out of his tiny swim trunks. God, everything about him kept Portland hot. "Damn. Look at my sexy husband."

Tarek's gaze swept down Portland's body. "No. I'm too busy looking at mine."

Thankfully, the lube was still on the bed from their last round. He tossed it to Tarek. "I want to watch you lube that sexy hole while I get out of these trunks."

With an evil grin, Tarek made a show of drawing up his knees and wetting his asshole. He kept his hands at an angle that wouldn't block Portland's view as he stretched and fingered himself. Portland stripped and stroked himself. A bead of pre cum leaked out.

Tarek rolled upward and licked Portland's cock, openly savoring the cum. "Maybe I should fuck my toy so I can suck this. You taste so good."

Portland would be damned if Tarek rode anything other than his dick. He took Tarek down. Portland wasn't gentle as he shoved his way inside, punishing Tarek for the suggestion. "Maybe you should fuck what?"

Tarek moaned but still tried to get sassy. "Don't tell me you're jealous of a toy. You're so much better."

Portland thrust. "You're damn right I am." He changed angles, proving he knew Tarek's body better than any damn toy.

Tarek scratched at the sheets beneath him, as if looking for a place to hold on.

Portland didn't show mercy. He rammed home his meat, fucking Tarek hard. Tarek took it with only moans and zero complaints. Then Tarek squeezed his forearms. Something dark inside him cleared. This was his husband. His beautiful, perfect in every way other half. He moved slower and kissed his angel, hoping Tarek felt his love. Tarek's fingernails dug into his skin and he pushed upward, silently asking for the rough treatment. His baby always got what he wanted. It seemed right now he wanted Portland to fuck him like he hated him. He didn't let Tarek down. Over and over, Portland pounded his ass. He lost track of everything except the tight asshole he serviced. Suddenly, that hole tried sucking him deeper. Portland lost his breath as Tarek's body stole his soul and cum hit him in the chest.

Sounds tore from Portland. The waves of pleasure that rocked him made everything else disappear. When he collapsed on Tarek, wheezing and fighting for his life, Tarek accepted his weight without complaint.

"Fuck." *Wheeze*. "I'm too old. You'll kill me."

Tarek's body shook with laughter beneath him.

"You're laughing?" *Wheeze*. "Remind me to spank you later."

"Mmm. Promises. Promises."

Yeah. His new husband would be the death of him. Just the thought of spanking Tarek had him halfway ready to go again. "Just give me a second to recover."

Tarek ran his fingers through Portland's hair. His lips brushed the shell of his ear. "Stay right here as long as you want. I'll hold you together."

Portland's breath caught at the statement. It hit him. Tarek always held him together. Not just while he caught his breath, but through every aspect of life. He was the glue for Portland's sanity and heart. That was how he had recognized Tarek as his soulmate the first moment they met. It was the immediate soothing of his soul.

"I'll be your home." That was all Portland had to offer. He could and would keep Tarek safe and nourished. Cherished. They each had what the other needed. It was almost funny now when he looked back at how they had begun. He had thought he had Tarek duped. Portland had honestly believed he could trick the guy into always being by his side. All along, the joke was on him. They were each other's perfect match.

Keep an eye out for the next Atlantic City's Most Wanted, *Twice the Problems*

About the Author

CHARITY PARKERSON IS AN award-winning and multi-published author with several companies. Born with no filter from her brain to her mouth, she decided to take this odd quirk and insert it in her characters. One of her greatest loves is writing morally gray characters. You'll find them scattered throughout her hundreds of titles.

*Nine-time Readers' Favorite Award Winner

*2015 Passionate Plume Award Finalist

*2013 Reviewers' Choice Award Winner

*2012 ARRA Finalist for Favorite Paranormal Romance

*Five-time winner of The Mistress of the Darkpath

Connect with her online:

*Sign up for her newsletter: https://bit.ly/charityparkersonnewsletter

*Join her readers' group on Facebook: http://bit.ly/CharitysTribe

*Website: https://www.charityparkerson.com

*A list of her social media accounts and giveaways all in one place: http://hy.page/charityparkerson

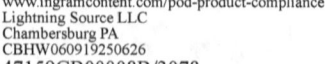